Paul Heatle and in prin including Tl HandJob, Horror Sleaze Trash, and Shotgun Honey, among others. He is the author of six novellas available for Kindle from Amazon, and is a regular contributor to R2 Magazine. He lives in the north east of England.

"Set in Heatley's native North East, this is a grim, gripping thriller that oozes nastiness throughout. The narrative is enjoyably queasy, and splattered with regular doses of brutal, bloody violence"
— **Tom Leins,** *author of Skull Meat : A Paignton Noir Mystery*

"...This reminds me of George Higgins--dialogue crackling with tension perfectly capturing the way working class criminals talk...."
— **Christopher Rhatigan,** *author of Race To The Bottom*

By the same author

AN EYE FOR AN EYE

Book 1 from the
'An Eye For An Eye' series

By Paul Heatley

Close To The Bone
An imprint of Gritfiction Ltd

Dedication
For Aidan.
And for Amy Linh, Jackson George, and Eliza Sue

An Eye For An Eye

Prologue

It was after-hours, but the landlord knew Jasmine's father and so the group was given free reign. He'd left the keys on the bar and gone up to bed, asked them to lock the door on their way out and slip them back through the letterbox. He hadn't been happy about it, but like most folk he knew not to say no to Neil Doyle's daughter.

The five occupied the back room, where the pool table and the dart board were. They helped themselves to drinks from behind the bar and were running up a hell of a tab they had no intention of paying back.

Richie Connell and Charlotte Donoghue played pool. Richie had rolled up the sleeves of his shirt and unbuttoned his collar, had a cigarette dangling from the corner of his mouth. It was hot in the backroom, it had made his hair wet. He slicked it from his forehead. He chalked his cue.

"You look like you're in a movie," Charlotte said.

Richie grinned. "You ever seen *The Hustler*?"

Charlotte scrunched up her face. "Eh?"

"Just makin sure you're warned, like."

"You're losin, mate. Let's get on with it, eh?"

"Aye, I'm losin right now, but these next few shots are gonna be magic." He put the chalk down, lined up his shot. He took his time. The white hit the sidewall, managed to tap one of his reds. He frowned. "Shite, man."

Charlotte laughed. "Fuckin magic, mate, *pure* magic."

Daniel Moore played darts with Carl Brown. He watched Charlotte's next shot, watched her pot two more yellows then line up for the black. "She's the hustler, mate," he said to Richie. Charlotte was Daniel's girlfriend. They'd been together six months, but they'd known each other since school. "Her dad took her with him to the pub every Saturday and Sunday when she was a bairn. This is what they did. Bet she didn't tell you that."

Richie sucked in his cheeks as Charlotte potted the black to win the game. "Nah, mate. She didn't."

"Nah, she never told me the first time we played, neither."

Charlotte grinned. "Just be grateful you didn't put any money on it. You wanna go again?"

"Y'kna what, pet?" Richie said. "*Aye.* Aye I fuckin do wanna play again. Kna what I'm up against this time, see? Now I'm not gonna go easy on you, like I did. Not gonna give you a chance."

"I'm sure it'll make all the difference," Charlotte said. She winked at Daniel and he smiled.

Carl slapped Daniel's arm with the back of his hand to get his attention. "Howay then, never mind what they're doin. You're getting your arse kicked over here, try concentrating on that."

Daniel turned back to the board. "It's not over yet." He threw his darts.

Carl shook his head. "Might as well be. Fucking hell man, how much you had to drink?"

"I've only had a couple."

"Maybe you should have a couple more then, you might throw it a bit straighter than you do when you're sober. Here, Charlotte – does he always have this much trouble hittin' the target?"

Richie laughed. Daniel raised an eyebrow.

"There's no complaints on my end," Charlotte said.

"How big's the target, like?" Carl said.

Daniel lowered the dart, turned to Carl. "Now hey – that's enough of that, eh?"

Carl raised his arms, backed off, but he was grinning. "Just kiddin with youse, mate."

"Aye, well, watch what you say, eh?"

"You just throw them fuckin' darts, eh?"

Jasmine Doyle sat at the bar. She sipped a gin and played on her phone, barely listened to her friends. She'd met a lad in one of her dad's clubs the weekend before, they'd been texting back and forth every day since and she was waiting on a message back. She checked the time, saw it was after two. Probably he was away to bed, but he could have told her as much rather than just leave her hanging on for a response that wasn't coming. She was starting to get annoyed, thought about sending him a message that said as much, but she didn't. She put her phone down, decided she would give him a chance to explain himself in the morning. She finished the gin and turned to the room. It was late, but she wasn't tired. Bored, but not tired.

Richie, halfway through losing another game, leaned his cue against the wall and popped his spine. He went behind the bar, poured himself a drink. "You want anything?" he said to Jasmine.

She passed him her glass. "Same again."

"Howay, Richie," Charlotte said. "Don't drag it out. Just come be a man and get it over with."

"That what you said to Dan the first time?" Carl said.

"Here," Daniel said. "I'm not gonna tell you again."

"Lighten up, man," Carl said. "Y'kna it's just a bit of banter."

"Nah, you're bein' an arsehole. I've telt you to stop, so just stop."

Jasmine watched them. She took the glass Richie offered her and drank. "Nah man, Carl," she called across the room. "The first time, she says *Is that it?*"

Daniel and Carl looked at her. Daniel's face dropped. Carl laughed. "You know what she said after that, right?"

"*It in yet?*"

Carl laughed harder.

Charlotte sucked her teeth. She gripped the pool cue, her knuckles white. Behind the bar, Richie covered his mouth with his drink, tried to hide his smirk.

"All right, all right," Daniel said. "You've all had a laugh. Let's leave it off, now."

"You sound like you're taking it all very personally, Dan," Carl said. "It's just a laugh, mate."

"You really got a small dick, Dan?" Jasmine said. She turned to Charlotte. "How big's it, Charlotte? You don't have to say anything, just use your hands so we get an idea."

"What're you winding him up for?" Charlotte said.

"Whey, it's like Carl said, it's just a bit of banter, Charlotte." Jasmine's eyes twinkled maliciously, they way they did when she took the piss and knew full well her target wouldn't say a thing against her. "And you haven't answered. I mean, the fact you won't say *anything* about it, that's got me worried for you, girl. Are you unsatisfied? I mean, you reckon that's why she's so good at pool, Richie? All that pent-up sexual frustration, she's just *whacking* them balls?"

Richie's smile faded. He looked like he didn't want

to get involved.

"Just lots and lots of practise," Charlotte said.

Daniel threw a dart. It hit the board, number twenty.

"Nearly a triple," Carl said. "Howay, Danny boy – looks like you play better when you're pissed off."

Daniel set his jaw, didn't answer. He took aim. Carl blew on his ear right before he released. The throw went wild. The dart embedded itself in the wall.

Daniel wheeled on Carl, swung a punch. Carl ducked it, laughing. "Oh, aye, Dan! Getting feisty!" He gave Daniel a shove.

Daniel still had a dart. His fist was shaking around it. "I'm fuckin warnin' you, mate."

Carl spread his arms. "What're you gonna do, eh? Howay man, *what* are you gonna fuckin *do*?"

"I'm warnin' you –"

"I'm hearing a lot of warnings, Dan, but you're not doin *shit*." He shoved him again, danced back as Daniel threw another punch.

"Just leave it, Dan," Charlotte said. "You an'all, Carl."

"Howay, lads," Richie said, still behind the bar. "That's enough now. It's all jokes, aye?"

Jasmine sat on her stool, laughed. She glanced at her phone, but still no response. She turned back to Daniel and Carl.

Daniel's face was turning red. "Right, leave off, or I swear I'll smash your fuckin' face in."

"Howay, big lad." Carl danced like a boxer. "Can you fight your own fights when your fatha's not round?"

"Here, I divvint need me dad to kick your fuckin' teeth in!"

"Why aye – you can't even touch us, man." He

pushed Daniel again, shoved his right arm, then tapped him on the side of the head with a closed fist.

Daniel grabbed for him. "Fuckin' arsehole!" Spit flew from his lips. He swung wildly. Carl bounced backwards, out of his reach, but then he hit the stool next to Jasmine and came to a stop, startled. Daniel caught him up, landed a punch to his chest with his left fist.

Jasmine laughed. "Give him another one, Dan! You heard what he was saying about you! We all heard it!"

Carl clutched at where the blow had landed. "*Ow*, man, y'fuckin cunt!"

Daniel swung for him with the dart. Carl saw it coming. He ducked, dropped to the floor. Daniel's momentum carried him through. His fist connected with something hard and his hand opened, he twisted against the impact and stumbled, fell. When he looked back he saw Carl and Richie wide-eyed, staring at Jasmine. She sat on the stool still, her hands raised, shaking. The dart was in her right eye. She screamed.

1

Graeme Taylor woke, rolled onto his side and checked the time. It was just after eight. He groaned. When last he'd checked the clock it had been after half-three. Sleep was coming to him harder and harder, and staying with him for less and less time. He'd heard it said that as people grew older it was common for insomnia to plague their nights, but he was only fifty-three. He'd thought that it applied to the over-sixties.

From experience, he knew that was that, he was awake, and there was no point staying in bed any longer. Kicking the blanket back, he rolled out and landed on all-fours, thought about doing some push-ups, thought better of it, then got to his feet and dragged himself along to the bathroom to take a long piss. As he washed his hands he inspected his face in the mirror. His wrinkles were deep, his dark hair was greying, and his stubble was starting to come in white. Running a knuckle along his jaw he listened to it scrape, but decided against a shave.

Stepping back, he gave the rest of himself a once-over. He slept in a pair of old underwear with holes in the crotch and seat, and a stained vest that was far beyond needing a wash and was really only fit to be binned. He patted his burgeoning waistline, then sucked it in. When he held his breath he still looked like he was in shape, but he had to promptly let it all back out and gasp air. He regretted foregoing the push-ups, but he still didn't do them. He coughed hard, cleared his chest and throat, spat a lump of thick green phlegm into the sink. It slithered quickly down the drain, but he ran the tap regardless to help it on its way.

The kitchen cupboards were bare, so he dressed and went out. His flat was in a high-rise, fourth from the top, and it was a long way down. The elevator was bust, had been for a long time. The building's caretaker used to say he was waiting for a part, but he'd always made his excuses without much enthusiasm, and it had gotten to the point nobody bothered to ask him anymore. They just got used to the stairs.

Graeme stopped for breath when he reached the foyer, leaned against graffiti-decorated walls, then went out. The sky was grey and he felt raindrops lightly tap his face. Despite the weather, he decided to forego the car and walked along the road, to the café. It wasn't far.

It hadn't been open long by the time he got there, but already a few tables were occupied. Older folks mainly, fellow insomnia-sufferers up with the dawn and waiting round for everyone else to wake, too. They, at least, looked like they were over sixty. There were a couple of younger men too, taxi drivers, meaty paws wrapped around deep-filled stotties that oozed tomato sauce and dripped egg yolk down their chins.

The bell above the door rang as Graeme stepped inside. Shannon was behind the counter. She looked up at the noise, saw him and smiled. "Morning, Graeme," she said. "How're you, pet?" Shannon was roughly the same age as Graeme, and had owned the café for the last ten years. Graeme had been visiting it for almost as long. She had bottle-blonde hair cut short and spiked, and skin leathery from frequent trips to the local sunbeds and abroad to Benidorm. Each ear held a looped gold earring.

"Not bad, Shaz, not bad." Graeme stepped up to the counter, pressed his hands down flat on top of it. "How's yourself?"

"Keeping busy. How about you? Got much on?"

"Nowt, at the minute."

"You all right? You look a bit pale."

He waved off her concern. "Just not sleeping too well is all."

"Guilty conscience?" She said it wryly, winked at him.

Graeme spread his arms, cocked his head. "What have I got to feel guilty about?"

They laughed together.

"What can I get for you this morning, love?"

Graeme eyed the menu above her head, but he already knew what he wanted. "Think I'll have a coffee and a bacon sarnie, the day."

"Not be long, pet, just have yourself a seat."

Graeme sat at a table opposite an old guy sipping tea. A dog lay on the ground by his feet, an old sheepdog with shaggy grey fur. It arched its eyebrows to look up at Graeme, then went back to staring at dirt on the floor. The old guy nodded, then turned back to his paper. He wore his coat still, but through the gap where it wasn't buttoned Graeme could see that he was wearing medals. There were three of them. He was too far and they were too concealed for him to make out what they were for, but even up close he wouldn't have been much the wiser.

One of the taxi drivers near the door stood up and wiped his mouth with a napkin, left. The bell rang. The other taxi driver had finished eating but he stayed where he was, leaning forward in his seat with his hands locked together, pressed against his forehead. Graeme could see his feet tapping under the table like he had a lot on his mind.

A woman sat two down from Graeme, near the window. Her long hair was losing its colour, and her body had lost its shape. She adjusted her glasses, stirred her tea, and let out a long sigh through her nostrils. She lifted a leg and tried to pass wind subtly, but it squeaked against the plastic chair.

Before he could take in the rest of the faces and demeanours present, Shannon brought Graeme his breakfast. "Here you go, young'un. Get that down ya."

"Cheers, Shaz." Graeme lifted the lid on the bun, covered the bacon with tomato sauce. He poured three sugar sachets into his coffee and stirred it, then took a sip. It scalded the roof of his mouth, burnt his throat all the way down. He coughed, cleared his throat, tasted phlegm. He picked up the sandwich and began to eat. Every so often he had to pull a bit of fat from between his teeth, deposit it on the corner of the plate. His eyes roamed the café, watched the old guy continue reading his paper, his medals jangling under his coat whenever he moved, watched the lady two tables down staring out the window. She didn't pass anymore wind. The other taxi driver took his hands from his face and stood up, pulled his jacket off the back of the chair and left. A couple more people came in, ordered, left. They didn't sit. The phone rang and Shannon took an order, and ten minutes later a young lad in oily overalls appeared to pick them up.

Graeme finished his sandwich, nursed his coffee. As he began to contemplate his plans for the day, of which he had none, he became aware of his phone buzzing in his pocket. It vibrated against his thigh. He pulled it out, checked the caller ID. It was Neil Doyle, but it was his home number. Graeme frowned. Usually he called from one of his clubs, or the gym, or his own mobile phone. He rarely called from home, and had made it perfectly clear that under no circumstances was anyone ever to call him there. Graeme took another quick mouthful of coffee, answered. "Hello?"

"Is this Graeme Taylor?"

It wasn't Neil's voice. "Aye?"

"All right, Graeme? We need you to get on over to the house, mate. Like, fuckin *pronto*."

Graeme scratched his cheek. "Somethin up, like?"

"I wouldn't be callin ya if there wasn't, would I?"

"Anythin to be worried about?"

"Nah — but look man, I've still gotta make some calls once I get off with you, so just get your arse over here, aye? And get a shifty on."

"Uh-huh."

"Got that?"

"Aye."

"Fuckin *mint*. Fast as you can, like." The caller hung up.

Graeme looked at the phone a moment before putting it back in his pocket. He drained off what remained of his cooled coffee and got to his feet.

"You off, Graeme?" Shannon said.

He nodded. "That's me away."

"Big plans for the day?"

He shrugged. "Just have to wait and see."

***

Neil Doyle lived in Jesmond. Graeme hurried back to the high rise to get his car, then drove over. Halfway there it started to rain, thick drops crashing down upon the windscreen, but by the time he reached the house it had stopped. The clouds, however, remained dark and promised another downpour.

The kerbs were lined with cars and it took Graeme a while to find a space to park. He started to wonder how many of the cars belonged to neighbours, and how many were there to see Doyle. He'd only ever been to the street a couple of times before, and he couldn't remember it ever being so busy in the past. A nervous fluttering began in the pit of his stomach, a worry that maybe something was up, something had happened that potentially put them all in danger, everyone in any way associated with Doyle and his various enterprises throughout Newcastle.

On his way to the house he checked the time. It had been over half an hour since he'd received the call. Traffic and rain had slowed him, but if as many of the vehicles were there for Doyle as he suspected they were, he doubted anyone would notice him slipping in at the back of the gathering, a little late.

The house, like all the houses on the road, was big. Three storeys high, seemingly every room with a bay window. It was an affluent neighbourhood, the residents all bankers and accountants and the like. If they knew who Neil Doyle was, they kept it to themselves and accepted the given story that he owned a string of nightclubs and gyms.

Graeme went up the path that cut the front garden in two, made for the front door. There were two guys there already, smoking. They saw him approach, greeted him by name. Graeme was sure he'd probably met them before, but most of the men Doyle surrounded himself with were of the same ilk: broad shouldered and bald-headed, and he could never tell them apart. He nodded, said "Lads," and went inside.

The house was full. Graeme recognised a number of faces milling about in the hallway, others through in the kitchen and in the front room. Some of them acknowledged him, but mostly everyone seemed tense, nervous. They made small-talk amongst themselves, but it was strained. Doyle wasn't anywhere to be seen.

The full spectrum of Doyle's varied associates were present. The juice-heads in tight t-shirts and vests that attended the gym run by his son Michael; the fellow businessmen with whom Doyle had working arrangements, kitted out in their finest, ostentatious grey, black, and blue three-piece suits with perhaps a handkerchief protruding from a breast pocket, or the chain of a pocket-watch hanging from another; and the lowest-rung employees, the street-level dealers with their tracksuit bottoms tucked into their socks, and polo shirts that flaunted their thin arms, and accents like someone was trying to strangle the Geordie out of them. Graeme had never seen such a mismatched bunch all squeezed into one space before. He noticed, with a mix of both pride and disappointment, that there was no one else there like him; a middle-aged guy with fading jeans, scuffed boots, and an old leather jacket shrugged over a black shirt.

A door off the hallway, near the foot of the stairs, opened and Michael Doyle stepped out. The gathering, already fairly quiet, fell silent. Michael rolled his shoulders, looked round. "Right," he said, his voice deep enough to shake the walls. "If you know what you should be doing, get to it. See or hear anything, straight on the fucking phone. Off you go." Most of the room filed out. Michael saw Graeme. "Howay," he said, tilting his head back through the door into the room behind him. Graeme forced his way through the exiting throng.

Michael took him into the study, then closed the door. One wall was made up of filled bookshelves, tomes that Graeme imagined were there more for decoration than for anyone to actually read. Directly in front of him was a floor to ceiling window which, on a brighter day, would be sure to let in plenty of light, and to his right there was a desk, against which leaned Neil Doyle. To his left there was a sofa. Someone was sitting on the sofa, a young lad Graeme didn't recognise. Whoever he was, he looked nervous. His hands were clasped tightly between his thighs and he chewed on his bottom lip. He stared at everything with wide eyes, stared at Graeme, flinched when Neil began to speak.

"What've you heard?" he said.

Graeme shrugged. "Nowt," he said.

Neil pushed himself off the desk, straightened up and crossed his arms. The kid on the sofa flinched again. Graeme frowned, wondered who he was, why he was present.

Michael left Graeme's side, slowly circled the room, stood behind the sofa. The kid jittered, tried to roll his eyes far enough back to see Michael, what he was doing there, without actually turning his head. Michael crossed his arms in imitation of his father. Unlike Neil, who since making the venture into 'legitimate' business never wore anything other than a tailored suit, he wore a tight black t-shirt that showed off his arms, the bulging, rippling muscle there that throbbed beneath the surface like there were snakes under his skin.

"Jasmine's in hospital," Neil said.

"Well, shit," Graeme said, unsure what else he could say. He hadn't had much to do with Jasmine Doyle, and he was grateful. Whereas Michael was his own man and handled his own business, Jasmine had earned a reputation as a spoilt princess. From what little Graeme had seen, it wasn't unwarranted. "Sorry to hear that. It serious?"

"Oh, it's pretty fucking serious," Neil said. He took a deep breath. "She's lost an eye."

Graeme blinked. "An eye?"

"Yes."

"An *eye?*"

"*Yes.*"

"Bloody hell. How the fuck'd that happen?"

"Out last night with some mates. They were in the back of some pub after-hours, having drinks, playing pool, and a couple of the lads got into a scuffle. She got in the middle of it, one of the twats had a dart in his hand, stuck it in her eye." Graeme could see the way Neil trembled with barely contained fury. The kid on the sofa could see it, too. "She's in the hospital now. Her mother's there with her."

"Hang on, hang on – he stuck it in her eye?" Graeme said. "On purpose?"

"She says it happened too fast, she can't remember." Neil turned to the kid. "You were there, you tell him."

The kid almost shit himself when he was spoken to. He stammered, then settled himself down and cleared his throat. "Uh, well, it was –" He coughed. Graeme could see beads of sweat forming on his forehead. "Dan and Carl were scrapping on, and I guess they just, like, got too close to her, y'kna?" The kid looked at Graeme like he expected him to say something.

Graeme blinked. "All right," he said.

Neil looked at the kid. His eyes narrowed. "What's your name again?"

"Um – it's Richie, sir. Richie Connell."

"Right." He spoke to Graeme. "There was four of them there with Jasmine, they all legged it apart from Richie here. He called the ambulance, went with her to the hospital, and you see how he's sitting there? Sitting there like he's gonna piss himself."

Richie swallowed.

"I mean, what's he think he's done wrong? He's done everything right. Unless there's something he's not telling us."

"Must be scared of you, dad," Michael said.

Richie gave a start at the voice behind him.

"Must be. But what's he got to be scared about? Did you stick the dart in her eye?"

He shook his head fast, as if terrified he was about to be accused. "No! I mean, uh, no, sir."

"Then why're you so worried?"

"Scared for his mates," Michael said.

"Maybe. But one of them mates has gone and blinded my little girl. Who did it?"

Richie's jaw worked, but no words came out.

Neil raised an eyebrow. "Howay, son, it wasn't a difficult question. You were there. You saw it happen."

Richie coughed hard like there was something lodged in his throat he needed to get loose before he could speak again. "I-I-I don't know, sir, I don't know who did it. They were fighting, and it was an accident. They didn't mean to do it."

"Maybe not. But they *did* do it. It's done. Apologies aren't gonna grow her fuckin eye back, are they? What happened?"

"I don't know, sir, I swear down. Like Jasmine said, it all happened so fast – I didn't even know anyone was holding a dart!"

Neil stared at Richie. Richie couldn't hold his gaze. He turned away, lowered his eyes to the ground. His lips trembled like he was about to cry and his thighs pressed closer together like he really was about to piss himself.

Neil turned to Graeme. "Here's the crack. I've made everyone that needs to know aware of the situation. Wanted them to hear it from me before they could hear it from anywhere else. And I also wanted them to know that it's business as usual. If anyone sees the two, they're gonna give us a shout, but chances are they're both gonna stay indoors, off the streets. Lookit, I'm not gonna gan on the warpath, tearing up the Toon looking for these little cunts, not unless I have to. I wanna get them in, find which one it was, and get it dealt with. Quick and quiet. Did you catch them names he said?"

Graeme thought. "Dan and Carl, wasn't it?"

"Aye. You know who Dan is?"

"Should I?"

"Daniel Moore. As in son of Robert Moore. As in nephew of Patrick Moore."

"Fuckin hell."

"Exactly."

"What about the other one?"

"What about him?"

"Family?"

"Nae idea. What's his last name?" He asked Richie.

Richie squeaked. "Brown," he said.

Neil pulled a face. "None the wiser," he said.

"He's from Middlesbrough," Richie said. "They're in Middlesbrough still. His family, I mean."

Neil raised an eyebrow. "You're telling us that now? D'you not think that's maybe somethin you should've told us straight away? What if this lad's done a flit back down to Boro, man! Did you think about that?"

Richie was pale. "He doesn't – he won't – they don't get on. He was stashing drugs in his bedroom, under the bed, but he had a baby sister and she found a pill on the carpet. She didn't take it, like, but his parents went mental, kicked him out. He won't go back there. He'll still be in Fenham."

"I'll tell you what, son, he'd fuckin better be." Neil

glared at Richie a moment longer, then continued on to Graeme. Graeme could see the tension in his face, in his shoulders. Could see the way he battled to stay calm, or at least as calm as he was usually able to present himself. "Michael's going after Dan. He's gonna bring him in. If we need to have any trouble with his dad or uncle, I want it dealt with as quickly as I want the rest of this sorted. You're gonna gan fetch Carl. Richie here'll give you the address. And if he's not there, if he's not in Fenham, then it looks like you're going down to Boro."

"All right. I'll want someone with us, though."

"Aye. Take one of the lads outside."

Graeme didn't want to use one of the skinheads. "I've already got someone in mind."

"Who?"

"Tony Gordon."

Neil thought on the name.

"Had the straightener with him a few months ago, didn't I?" Michael said.

"Tracksuit Tony?" Neil said.

"Aye," Graeme said.

"The fuck you want him for?"

"Cos the lad might run," Graeme said. "I don't run."

"Well just grab one of the lads outside man, for fuck's sake!" Neil's level mask was slipping.

"Tony's a good lad," Graeme said. "I know him, I like him, I trust him."

Neil waved his arms. "Whatever, man! Go get him and just get on with it then, eh? And bring Carl fucking Brown of Middlesbrough straight back here."

"Aye." Graeme went to the desk, picked up a pen and paper, gave it to Richie. "Write down the address, son," he said. "Memory's not great." While Richie scribbled the details, Graeme spoke to Neil. "What're you gonna do to him, whichever one it was?" He wasn't sure he wanted to know. Killing the kid seemed excessive, but knowing Neil's temper, and how capable he was of winding himself up, he wouldn't be surprised if that was the plan.

Neil leaned against the desk again, refolded his arms. His face turned dark, his eyes were very hard and focussed, all his calm came back. "When I find out who it was," he said, "I'm gonna take one of his fuckin eyes."

2

Graeme called Tony from the car, found out he was in the gym, drove over there. He was lifting weights when Graeme arrived. Graeme stood by the bench, waited until he had finished his set. Tony sat up, grabbed a towel, mopped the sweat from his face. "All right?" he said. The clang of barbells and dumbbells, the scrape of cable machines, the constant thud and whir of treadmills filled the air, and over it all a repetitive techno beat that couldn't quite drown out the frequent grunts and groans of the labouring men and women.

"Not bad, son, not bad," Graeme said. "Were you at work last night?"

Tony was a bouncer. "Aye. Got off at three."

"Still a bit early in the day, isn't it?"

"Well, it's not gonna build itself, is it?" He flexed a bicep, then laughed. "What can I do for you, anyway?"

"Need a hand with somethin."

"What?"

"Nothin much. Just need you to come along."

"What is it?"

"Just pickin some kid up. Nothin to it."

"Nowt to it, eh? Why don't you just tell us *all* the crack then and I'll make me own mind up?"

"Neil Doyle's daughter took a dart to the eye. Two lads involved, on me way to pick one of them up and take him back to the big man."

Tony raised an eyebrow, folded his arms. "So the little tart took a dart. What do I care? She got me a kicking not so long ago."

"You're all healed now, though, eh?"

"Not the point, Graeme."

"Just a few bruises here and there, it was nothing serious."

"She's a little cunt, man. She lost the eye?"

"From what I've heard."

Tony shrugged. "Y'kna what, I'd like to say I feel bad for the lass, but I really divvint. Two lads stuck a dart in her eye? She's lucky they didn't take an eye each. The way she gans on, someone was always gonna give her a clip eventually."

"The lads were fighting, she got in the middle."

"Aye, and what were they fighting about? Bet she had something to do with it."

"Don't know what they were fighting about, don't know which one stuck the dart in. To be honest, I don't really care. But Neil cares, and he wants to know."

"This has got nowt to do with me, Graeme."

"I know it hasn't, but I'm askin you to come along. As a favour."

"A favour to you, or to me?"

"Well, y'kna I've done plenty for you."

"Not denying it."

"The Doyle's respect you, Tony. Since the straightener. You took your licks, and you got a few in, you haven't grumbled and you were back at work the next week. You took it like a man, and that impressed them."

Tony shrugged. "It was two weeks after. And their respect didn't pay back the wages I lost that fortnight I had to take off cos me eyes were swollen shut and I couldn't breathe through me fuckin nose. And that was cos of his daughter. I had to have a fuckin fight with Michael Doyle because I wouldn't let her in a club when she was already smashed out of her head? I had to take a beating because I was doing me fuckin job? Oh aye, I'm proper glad they were impressed, like. Makes it all the better, really does."

"Howay, Tony. For me, man."

Tony ran his tongue round the inside of his mouth, said nothing.

"Look, one of the lads…" Graeme stepped closer, lowered his voice. "One of them, not the one I'm goin to pick up, the other one, he's Robert Moore's son."

Tony didn't recognise the name.

"You might not have heard of him, but you've probably heard of Patrick Moore, aye?"

"Mm."

"Well, Robert's his brother. And they're just as bad as each other, believe me. Anyway, I've got a nasty feeling, right? If things go bad – and I mean, touch wood that they won't – but if they *do*, and this thing turns bigger, I want someone with me that's gonna watch me back, and know I'll do the same for them. I want you, Tony. I trust you."

Tony's shoulders sagged. "Christ's sake man, Graeme…"

"I wouldn't ask just anyone."

Tony sighed. It was long and exaggerated. "Right. *Fine*. Aye, I'll do it. But only for you, right? I couldn't give a toss about the fuckin Doyle's. I'll come along because I trust you, because we go back. And I'll do it for me fuckin mother, an'all, cos God knows if she found out you asked us for a favour and I said *No* I'd never hear the bloody end of it."

Graeme smiled. "That's all I ask, mate. How is your mother, by the way?"

Tony shot him a look. "Watch it."

Graeme laughed. "Aye. Howay then, let's get going."

"Right. But I've gotta shower first."

"Quick as you can."

"Aye." Tony turned, but Graeme stopped him.

"You got a change of clothes?"

"Course I have."

"Anythin that's not a tracksuit?"

Tony frowned.

"They still call you Tracksuit Tony. I mean, it's been so long now it's probably always gonna stick, but it wouldn't hurt to turn up in some pants every once in a while, or even a pair of jeans."

Tony sucked his teeth. "You're trying me patience now, mate."

Graeme grinned. "Maybe. But y'know I've only got your best interests at heart."

***

Tony had a pair of jeans and a blue t-shirt and he wore them instead of his usual tracksuit. The moniker *Tracksuit* had stuck as it became apparent to people what a fitness freak he was, and was rarely seen out of his workout gear apart from when he was on the doors. Either in the gym or jogging along the banks of the River Tyne, Tony was always in his tracksuit.

He'd been a teenager when Graeme first met him, about thirteen. Even then he'd been much the same. He ran the cross-country for his school, went out for all the track events on the sport days, and usually won. Graeme had been going with his mother at the time. He'd turned to her one night when Tony was out, running in the woods near their house.

That lad of yours, he ever do anything else?

Ah, he enjoys himself. I leave him to it.

He not have any mates?

He has friends, he just prefers his own company. Especially when he's running.

It's a strange way for a lad his age to be.

Well, it was after his dad died, wasn't it? That's when he started with the running.

They left Tony's car at the gym and drove to Fenham in Graeme's. Tony took the wheel and Graeme gave directions. They pulled to the kerb outside the house. It was a terraced street, big old houses three-storeys high, much like Neil Doyle's though nowhere near as grand. They looked like student lets, and they probably were. A couple of young Asians passed the car, both female, chattering away in a language neither man could identify, and further down a young lad stepped out of his front door, pulled up his hood, and crossed the road. Other than these three, there was no one else to be seen.

"Let's give him a knock, then," Graeme said.

They got out the car. Loud music, drum-heavy, emanated from a house, muted by the walls, though it was impossible to tell which one. The faint smell of cigarette smoke hung on the air and, beneath that, weaker yet somehow more pungent, marijuana.

They went up the path leading to the front door. The garden was wild and overgrown, the grass almost covering the walkway. A microwave had been dumped into the miniature jungle, and a mini-fridge, and from the worn and rusted looks of them they had been there a while. "Keep an eye down the side," Graeme said. "Make sure he doesn't try to leg it out the back."

Tony went to the corner of the house and watched

while Graeme knocked. He put his ear near the door and listened for approaching steps, but heard none. He knocked harder, stepped back and looked up the front of the house, watched the windows. There was no activity. One of the windowsills on the second floor had been filled with empty beer bottles. "Anything your end?"

"Nothing," Tony said.

Graeme tried the handle. It was unlocked. He looked at Tony, shrugged, and they went inside.

They found someone in the kitchen. He sat at the table, facing them, eating unbuttered toast. The whole kitchen stunk of toast like nothing else had ever been prepared there. He gave a start when he saw Graeme and Tony in the doorway, dropped his crust. "What-what – who are you?"

"Your name Carl?"

The kid blinked. "Carl? No, I'm –"

"I couldn't give a toss, son. We've been knocking. You didn't hear us knock?"

The kid's eyes were red, his lids were heavy, and his skin was pale. If he wasn't high he was hungover, and probably couldn't hear much of anything outside his own head. "Uh, n-no, no, I didn't, sorry." He had a southern accent, wore clothes a size too small that clung tightly to his too-thin frame. His hair was styled into a pointed quiff, but it looked as if it had last been gelled a couple of days ago, as dry flakes clogged in it and drifted down past his face when he moved, like dandruff.

"Where's Carl?"

"I don't know if he's in."

"Anyone else in?"

"I don't know. I haven't been up long."

"Come here, son."

The kid didn't move, stayed on the seat, his eyes

wide. He reminded Graeme of Richie, of the terrified look on his face.

"Howay, son, on your feet and over here."

The kid stood up, took cautious steps.

"Show us where Carl's room is, eh?"

The kid nodded, then led them up two flights of stairs to the top floor. He pointed at another set of stairs. "He has the attic room," he said.

"Head on up and knock, then."

"He doesn't like any of us going up there."

"I don't give a shit what he likes. Here's the crack son – I don't know what Carl looks like, so until you prove otherwise, *you're* Carl, understand? And you're not leaving our fuckin sight. Now. Get on up, and we'll be right behind you."

The kid's mouth gaped, opened and closed a couple of times, then he turned and went up the stairs and Graeme and Tony followed. The door at the top was closed. The kid hesitated before he knocked. "Carl?" He called through the wood. "You in?"

The door flung open. "What do you want man, you little prick?" The kid flinched, then Carl flinched when he saw Graeme and Tony.

Graeme dragged the kid out the way, pushed Carl back into the room. Tony followed.

"Take a seat, mate," Graeme said. "Let's have a word."

The room stunk of sweat and wank. Dirty clothes were bundled in a corner next to a desk that had no papers, no notebooks, but was instead littered with tobacco fibres and looked to be where Carl rolled his cigarettes. His bed was unmade, the sheet was loose at one corner and there was a pillow on the floor. The walls were decorated with pictures of old punk bands, most of whom were flicking the V's, and posters of naked women, most of whom were blonde. Tony closed the door. On the back of it had been pinned a dozen or so gig tickets.

Carl sat at the desk. He was nervous, though not quite as terrified as Richie or the kid that had brought them up. "Carl Brown, aye?" Graeme said.

"Yeah." His voice was barely a whisper, all the earlier bravura when he had answered the door gone. He swallowed.

"Do you know who I am?"

Carl gnawed his lip. "I can guess who you're with."

"If that guess sounds like it has something to do with Jasmine Doyle, then you'd be right."

Tony stood by the door, said nothing. He leaned against the frame, blocked the exit, crossed his arms and stared at Carl.

"You a student, Carl?" Graeme said.

"Uh, no."

"But that other lad is, right?"

"Yeah."

"And this is a student house?"

"For the most part."

"So what do you do?"

"Uh, well –"

"You sell drugs, aye?"

"Aye."

"How many people live here with you and the other lad?"

"There's six of us altogether."

"Six, eh? Plenty of potential customers for you right there already. They bring round some friends – well, you must be rolling in it. No wonder you get to have the top floor room, eh? The one with the skylight!"

"Aye, aye, must be." Carl fidgeted.

"Bit of a grim day the day, though. Still, must be nice when the sun's out. Where're the other four housemates, then?"

"I don't know."

"Studying, you reckon?"

"I don't know."

"You hear this, Tony? None of them know where each other are. It's like they divvint even care about one another."

"How's Jasmine?" Carl said.

"Straight to business, are we? She's blind, son. Lost an eye. That's what happens when you get a fuckin dart in it. I mean, maybe it's just me, right, but I always thought it was smart to keep the pointy end of things away from a person's face, especially when that person's father isn't someone you want coming after you."

"Look, it wasn't me, right? I swear down, it was Dan, he had the dart, he was swinging it round! If he hadn't hit her he woulda hit me!"

"No one would've give a shit if he'd hit you, son."

Carl's jaw went slack. He didn't know what to say.

"Up you get. You're comin with us."

"I swear to you, man, I swear to God – I swear on me mother! It wasn't me! It was Dan, man! He took her fuckin eye out, it had nothing to do with me!"

"Keep yourself together, son. You're showing yourself up. And divvint try pullin that *swear on me mam* shite with me, from what I've heard you don't even get on with her, so that counts for fuck all. If you've got nowt to worry about, well then you can tell Doyle everything that happened and then you can be on your way."

Carl swallowed. He looked from Graeme to Tony.

"Trust us, son. As far as your options go, that's the best one you've got."

***

Tony drove them to Jesmond, to Doyle's house. Graeme sat in the back with Carl, made sure he didn't try to fling himself out the door while they were moving. The kid said nothing the whole drive. He thought about it, though. A couple of times he turned from the window, opened his mouth, but then decided against it and turned back to the window. His left leg bounced and he popped his knuckles over and over until they wouldn't pop anymore and he was just pulling on his fingers.

Richie was still there, on the sofa where they'd left him. His hands were still between his thighs. A couple of skinheads were watching over him, hovering in a corner of the room, conversing between themselves in quiet voices until Graeme and Tony walked in with Carl between them. The third skinhead that had been on the front door, who had let them in, went in search of Neil.

Richie and Carl looked at each other, but they said nothing.

"Take a seat next to your pal," Graeme said.

Carl crossed the room, sat down. He glanced at Richie again, then tried to adopt a more casual pose on the sofa, shifted his weight repeatedly until he finally decided on a wide-legged slouch, one arm draped over the back and the other over the arm. When Neil entered the room he sat bolt-upright, slapped his hands between his thighs the way Richie had.

"Mr Doyle!" he said. "Mr Doyle, sir, I –"

"Shut your fuckin mouth, you cunt!" Neil jabbed a finger. He hunched his shoulders and stared at Carl until Carl whimpered and looked at the ground. "You'll speak when you're fuckin spoken to, understand?"

Graeme could see the sinews working in Carl's cheek, the way his jaw was grinding like he was trying not to cry.

"I asked you a fucking question!"

Carl turned his face up, startled. He hadn't heard any question.

"*Do you understand?*"

"Y-yes, sir!"

"Right. Answer everything I ask. One word answers will do until I want otherwise. Did you blind my daughter?"

"What – *no*! No, I –"

"One word answers, you little twat! Did you blind her?"

"No."

"Who did?"

"Daniel."

"You swear?"

"Yes."

"You swear on your fucking *life*?"

"*Yes!*"

"Watch your fuckin tone with me!"

Carl cowered.

"Right. I want details. Tell me what happened."

"Uh –"

"*Uh* – spit it out, man!"

"Me-me and Dan got in a fight –"

"What about?"

"I can't – I can't – I don't remember –"

"You don't remember?"

"N-no –"

"You better remember."

"We were – I was – we were winding him up –"

"About what?"

"I don't –"

"You'd better."

"I was just taking the piss out of him, cos I was beating him at darts. And then we were winding him up, cos his lass was there, we were winding him up about the size of his dick –"

"Who was?"

Carl looked at Richie, but Richie wouldn't face him. "Me – me and Jasmine, we were winding him up in front of Charlotte –"

"Has he got a small dick?"

"I –I don't know, I really don't."

"You saying Jasmine does?"

"No! No, it was just banter –"

"*Banter?*"

"I mean, we were just winding him up, that was all, but he took it really personally – maybe he does have a little dick, I don't know!"

"Then what?"

"Dan had a dart, and he started swinging it, and he caught Jasmine – Richie would have seen! He can back me up!"

"Richie didn't see anything. Richie's as much use as tits on a fucking bull."

"It was – it was too fast –" Richie said.

"I'm not talking to you!" Neil said. "I'm talking to this one! What happened next?"

"That was it!" Carl said. "Dan stuck the dart in her eye, that was it!"

"What happened next?"

Carl's face went blank. He didn't understand.

Neil spoke through his teeth. "What happened *next?*"

"I ran."

"You ran. You all ran, apart from Richie. Why'd

you run?"

"I don't, I-I-I don't know, I-I don't – I was scared. Dan and Charlotte legged it first, and I didn't think about it. I just ran."

"Did you go with them?"

"No. We went in different directions."

"Where'd you go?"

"I went to Leazes Park, and I slept in a bush because I was too scared to go home, but then I thought no one knows where I live, so I went back this morning."

"There's always someone knows where you go, son. Remember that."

Carl clasped his hands tightly. He'd come to the end of his story, and he knew that whatever was coming next, he had no control over it.

Neil spoke to Richie. "Everything he said, that match up with what you *do* remember?"

Richie nodded vigorously.

"So you didn't do it, Carl, that's what you're saying?"

"I swear to God," Carl said. A tear ran down his cheek. He sniffed hard.

"Daniel Moore stuck the dart in her eye."

"Yes."

"All right. Okay." Neil nodded. He folded his arms and the rage finally went out of his body. Carl noticed. He wiped the tear from his face, rubbed his eyes dry and sniffed again. "You two heard him." Neil spoke to Graeme and Tony now. "You believe him?"

"I don't think he'd be daft enough to lie," Graeme said.

Neil looked Tony up and down, like it took him a moment to recognise him without the tracksuit. "What do you think?"

Graeme glanced at Tony. Tony held Neil's eye. "I reckon you already know whether you believe him or not."

Neil watched Tony a moment longer, then smiled. "Aye." He turned back to Carl. "I don't think you did it, son. I believe you."

The relief was visible on Carl's face. "Thank you, sir, thank you – look, if you need any help finding Dan –"

"You didn't stick the dart in her eye. But you do have responsibility in it. And I lay blame at your feet. Not all of it, mind. The rest is reserved for Daniel."

The tension returned to Carl, but Neil stayed relaxed.

"And I will have to punish you," Neil said.

"But I didn't, I didn't do –"

"One day, if you ever have kids of your own, you'll understand. But, here. Listen. I appreciate you coming in and not making a fuss. And I appreciate you clarifying some things. But if you lied to me in any way – well. Do I really need to continue?"

"I would never lie, Mr Doyle, sir –"

"Good." Neil offered his hand. Carl stared at it, perplexed, like he was being offered a grenade. Then, as one of the skinheads coughed, Carl came to life and took the hand, shook it. Neil didn't let go. "You have responsibility. And you have to be punished. You understand that, don't you?"

Carl squeaked.

Neil took his index finger, wrenched it back, snapped it. Carl screamed. Neil slapped him, cut the scream short, grabbed his middle finger and snapped that too then let go of his hand. Carl fell to his knees, stared at his twisted fingers.

Neil gave him a moment to scream it out. When he finally silenced, he told him, "Get out." Carl kept his face lowered, then fled from the house. He turned to Richie. "You too, you useless twat."

Richie leapt from the sofa, ran after his friend.

Neil took a deep breath through his nose.

Graeme shuffled his feet. He and Tony looked at each other. Tony raised his eyebrows. "So," Graeme said.

"So," Neil said.

"You, uh, you need us to hang round, or…?"

Neil crossed his arms, nodded.

Graeme sucked his teeth. "All right. What now?"

***

Graeme and Tony sat on the sofa. The skinheads had left.

"This is taking longer than I thought," Tony said.

Graeme had made himself comfortable. "It's taking about as long as I expected. They ask you to do one thing, you can bet you'll be dragged into doing the rest of it, too."

"Uh-huh. Well in that case this is taking longer than you led me to believe. You could've warned us of that before I said I'd come along."

"Well if I didn't say exactly that, I certainly alluded to it. You were touch and go as it was."

"Then thank heavens you lied to us, eh? Prick."

"There were no lies, sunshine. An omission of truth, perhaps, though I'm fairly certain I made mention that there was the potential it could go on for longer. Anyway, what you got to do that's better?"

"Anything, mate. Anything's better than sitting round on me fucking hands. What're we waiting for, anyway?"

"Waiting for Michael to check in with Dan."

"He's taking his time."

"What do you want me to tell you?"

"Here's something you can tell me – why you?"

"Eh?"

"Why's he roped you into this? There's plenty of other fuckers he can call on, isn't there? Thought you were living the quiet life."

"He likes to keep us busy from time to time."

"I'd maybe believe you if he didn't task you with tracking down the lad that mutilated his daughter. That's a canny personal thing to entrust just anyone with."

Graeme shrugged. "What do you want us to say?"

"Jesus Christ man, Graeme – I divvint want you to *say* anything, I just want you to stop being so bloody evasive and tell us the fucking crack, man. What's the reason?"

"It sounds like bragging. And I'm not the bragging kind."

"Aye, certainly, you're all humility. Just spit it out."

"Well, because I'm good at it. I don't get stuck in so much these days, but, aye. I'm good at it. At finding people. At finding things out. At sorting problems. And I can talk to people. I can get them to tell me things, things they won't tell others, answers to questions other people wouldn't think to ask. Because I know when to be friendly with them, and to tell them what they want to hear, and I know when to be scary. So, aye. That's why he keeps us round. That's why he keeps in touch. I'm good at what I do."

"Reckon that gives you a fuzzy feeling inside, does it? To know you're *valued*."

"You're valued too, y'kna."

"Aye, maybe to me mam. She still asks after you, by the way."

"Aye, you kind of mentioned that earlier. Thought she got married."

"She did. She still asks."

"I'm flattered. What do you tell her?"

"I tell her you live alone and you're getting fat and kicking you to the kerb when she did was the smartest thing she's ever done."

"I'm not so flattered anymore."

"I'm just kidding with you. I tell her you're doing fine. I lie, basically."

"I am fine. And for the record, she didn't kick me to the kerb. We mutually agreed that terminating our relationship was for the best."

"Whatever you say, mate."

"She's a good lass, your mam. Whoever she's with, he's a lucky bloke."

"Aye. She's always goin on at us, though. *Mind, that Graeme, he's done a lot for you. Divvint gan forgetting it.* So I tell her, don't worry mam, I can't forget, he likes to remind me himself every other week!"

"That's not true."

"Fair enough, every month then."

"Y'know, I've done things for you, opened some doors, but it's not like I'm bringing it up all the time."

"You might not state the acts by name, but you certainly bring them up. *Howay man, Tony, all I've done for you. Howay Tony, you still owe us this favour.* Sound familiar? And I mean, you got us the job on the doors, and I'm grateful, but how long's it gonna be until you reckon I've finally paid that debt off?"

"I've done plenty more for you besides, believe me. I've always looked out for you."

"You're not me dad, Graeme. I don't need you to look out for us."

The door to the study opened before Graeme could respond. It was one of the skinheads. "Howay," he said.

Graeme and Tony stood, followed him out. Neil was in the hallway, by the door with a couple of others.

"Get in your car," he said. "We're going to the gym." He looked at Tony. "You know the one."

"You got the lad?" Graeme said.

"Not exactly."

3

The gym belonged to Neil. It was seven in the evening, and it should have been open still, but they'd kicked the meatheads out and closed it early, locked the doors and drawn the blinds. Tony had been in it once before, under similar circumstances, and Graeme could see the memory of it playing over his tense features. Except this time he wasn't the one about to be thrown to the wolves – this time he *was* one of the wolves. And their victim, their prey, was a man Graeme hadn't seen in years: Robert Moore.

Robert was strapped to a chair in the centre of the gym, his mouth gagged. He was beaten and bloodied. His head lolled. He'd been stripped naked and tarpaulin had been spread on the mats beneath him. Small pools of blood had formed in the creases of the plastic and some, the ones directly under the chair, were still being filled. There was a steady drip sound like from a leaking tap. Michael and the skinhead he'd earlier left the house with were standing behind the chair. Michael's hands and forearms were red almost to his elbows. There was a tool bag open on the floor.

Neil clapped once. "So!" He took off his jacket and handed it to another skinhead, undid his cuffs and rolled up his sleeves. "Looks like you gave my boy a hard time. He's a big lad, is wor Michael, but he's placid. He's always open to reason. He wouldn't just go do something like this willy-nilly. You take a swing at him?"

Robert's head rolled on his shoulders. He blinked, tried to look at Neil, tried to sneer.

Neil grinned. He looked at Michael. "No Dan?"

"He wasn't there. Robert here says he hasn't seen him."

"You believe him?"

"No."

"He take a swing at you?"

"Aye. With a knife."

Neil raised an eyebrow. "That right, Robert? You tried to cut up my boy? Let me get this straight – your son blinds my daughter, and you think it's a good idea to try and stab my other kid? Jesus Christ, man. I always thought the Moore's weren't the brightest bulbs in the box, I just didn't realise how fucking dim they really were."

Graeme watched Robert. He was convulsing, and he started to wonder if he was choking. It soon became apparent he was laughing.

"Something funny, big lad?"

Robert threw his head back, continued to laugh through his gag.

Neil sucked his teeth. He nodded at Michael. Michael picked up a knife, stepped forward, cut the gag from Robert's mouth. He nicked his bottom lip in the process, and a line of bright red blood ran down his chin. Robert laughed harder, then his face turned mean and he spat blood. It landed on Neil's shoes. "Fuck you, you mouthy cunt!"

"Where's your son, Robert?"

"Fuck you!"

"Come on, you know the one. Lad called Daniel. You've probably seen him round a few times over the years."

"Fuck you!"

"The longer you draw this out, the worse it's gonna get for him."

"You think I'm gonna give up me boy?" Robert looked him up and down. "What kind of fitha do you think I am? What kind of fitha are *you*?"

"Me? I'm the kind that loves his children. The kind that cares for them, and protects them, and when someone does something to hurt them I'm gonna make sure they get hurt in turn. He needs to be punished, Robert. You can understand that. You say you don't, then you're a liar."

"If it'd been my bairn and not yours, what would you do? Would you give them up to me?"

Neil said nothing for a moment. "Restitutions are to be expected."

"Aye, but you hesitated, didn't ya? And that – what was that word? That makes it sound like you'd pay us off. You gonna let me pay you off? The way you're goin on, you want more. You're after blood."

"You can't buy back an eye."

"And you'd give me one of your kids'? You'd give us the big lad there's eye?"

"We're not going to discuss what-ifs and might-have-beens. What has happened, happened. Tell me where your boy is. I won't lie and say I'm not going to hurt him, because I am. But I won't kill him. And that's as good as you can get, isn't it?"

Robert ground his teeth.

"Tell us where he is, and it's over for you, too. We'll let you go. Maybe not straight away, but we'll stop with all of this."

Robert grinned with the corner of his mouth. "You haven't hurt us yet, you stuck-up cunt."

Neil held out his hand and Michael put the knife into it. He pressed it against Robert's chest. "Where is he?"

Robert looked past Neil, to Graeme and Tony. "Here, how many times can you tell one man to go and fuck himself before he gets the fuckin idea?" He was laughing again.

Neil grabbed a handful of his hair, ran the blade across his chest and opened his flesh. The blood began to run. Robert grit his teeth, strained against his binds. The legs of the chair began to rock and Michael put his hands on the back to hold it steady.

"Where is he?"

"That it? Is that it you fuckin fairy?"

Neil dropped the knife, laid in with his fists. He worked the body and face with hard and frequent blows, and Graeme saw him in his heyday, the street fighting man that took on all-comers, and usually won. He was wild like a pitbull, yet there was a control in his movements and his swings, like a dancer, like he could have been a boxer, one of the greats, if he hadn't been lured by the prospect of fast and easy ill-gotten cash. Robert's face turned black and blue. His cuts opened wider, he bled more. Sweat and spit flew from his mouth and forehead. Neil punched until his arms grew weary, then he grabbed Robert by the shoulders and screamed into his face. "*Where is he? Where the fuck is he?*"

Robert managed to laugh still.

"*Fucking tell me!*"

Robert spat blood in his face.

Neil hit him again. "*Where? Where? Fucking where, you piece of shit?*"

"Bring me your daughter, Neil!" Robert said. "Bring me your little girl, cos once I'm out of here I'm gonna take her other eye, and I'm gonna fuck the empty sockets!"

Neil grabbed the knife from the ground, stabbed Robert over and over. Blood flew, splashed, poured onto the tarpaulin. It went on and on. Graeme grit his teeth. Tony turned away.

Robert was dead, but the stabbing continued.

When Neil was done, he stepped back. He panted, tried to catch his breath. He dropped the knife. Robert's blood had painted him red from head to toe, covered him in gore. Graeme could see past him, could see Robert's corpse slumped in the chair. His stomach had been sliced wide open, his innards were hanging out, into his lap and down between his legs to the ground. Something, it might have been his liver, lay next to his foot.

Neil turned his face to the ceiling, closed his eyes. He spoke to no one in particular. "Clean it up."

4

Robert's body was cut and bagged. Graeme and Tony took Neil's boat down the Tyne after midnight, out to the North Sea.

Tony stood next to Graeme, held onto the railing though they weren't going fast. He sniffed his fingers. "Stink of blood," he said.

"It's the kind of thing that stays in your skin for a while," Graeme said. "And even when it's out, you're sure you can still smell it."

Tony sniffed again. "Aye." He'd helped at first, when the skinheads had started the dismemberment. When they'd brought out the electric saw, when limbs started being severed, when the smell got *really* bad, he'd had to step outside. He'd gone beyond pale, almost green. He hadn't thrown up, though. Graeme was glad of that, at least. The others would have ripped the piss if he'd thrown up.

Graeme took them out far on the water. It was a calm night. The surface was still, it rocked them gently. There were clouds in the sky, blocking the moonlight, but the lights from the boat were more than enough.

"Didn't know you could drive one of these," Tony said.

"Had to learn." Graeme dumped a package overboard. "You think this is my first time?" The bags were weighted. They made a big splash as they broke the water.

"Do I wanna know what time it *is*?"

"Nah, mate."

They took the boat back to the harbour, then drove to Jesmond, to Neil's. They slept on the sofa in the study and were woke early the next morning when Jasmine returned, assisted into the house by her mother.

Lydia Doyle was much younger than her husband. She wasn't Michael's mother, and had arrived on the scene a couple of years after the first Mrs Doyle's death from ovarian cancer. She'd been eighteen when Neil first met her, just turned, and was still eighteen when Jasmine was born. Jasmine was almost twenty, which meant she was older now than her mother had been at her birth. These days when the two were together they looked more like sisters than parent and child. Lydia wasn't exactly old, but she looked good – better than most other women her age. She'd lived a life of luxury, and it was apparent in her smooth, tanned skin, her toned curves under figure-hugging designer clothes.

That morning, though, she looked as if she had finally aged. The corners of her eyes were lined with crow's feet, and her lips were pinched into a thin, bloodless line. She held Jasmine by the elbow, guided her through the hallway.

Graeme and Tony stood in the doorway of the study. They, like the skinheads in the other doorways, tried not to stare, but couldn't help themselves. For the first time Graeme could remember, Jasmine wasn't done up. She wore a dishevelled tracksuit, her hair was tied back in a greasy ponytail. There was no make-up on her lowered face, and she wore a black eye patch that secured white padding to the wounded socket.

Jasmine tripped over her feet, almost fell. Lydia

caught her, kept her upright. Michael followed them through the house, carried his sister's overnight bag. He stood silent and solemn when they stopped, while Jasmine shifted her weight from foot to foot and sorted out her balance. Neil came down the stairs, rushed over. "You all right, pet? How you doing?"

Jasmine mumbled, didn't look up. They were standing still now, her mother holding one arm and her father the other, but she swayed. Graeme watched her. She squinted with her one eye, blinked a lot. He figured her depth perception was off.

Neil spoke to Lydia. "You just get back?"

"Aye, we just got back," she said. "Think you could do somethin about all these lads ogling her like she's in a fuckin zoo? What're they all doin here, anyway?"

Graeme tapped Tony on the arm and they stepped back into the room, out of sight. Neil snapped at his skinheads to get lost. The Doyle's stayed in the hallway. Tony returned to the sofa, sat down. Graeme stayed by the door, listened.

"What're you doing?" Tony said. He whispered. Graeme raised a hand to silence him.

"You're home now, pet," Neil said. "Come on, let's just get you upstairs."

When Jasmine spoke, her voice was very quiet. Graeme strained to hear. "I can manage, dad."

"All right, all right, just let your mam help you up them steps –"

"I'm not gonna fall, dad. I can manage it."

"That's it, just hold the banister."

"Neil, man!" It was Lydia's voice. "Leave the lass alone, will ya? She said she can manage. She doesn't need babied, for Christ's sake."

"Whey, she's lost the fuckin eye, hasn't she? That's

gonna take some adjustin, and I'm just tryin to help."

"Oh, aye, just shout it out why don't ya? She's not likely to fuckin forget, is she? And we all kna what you're just tryin to do, and she says she can manage."

"Will yous stop arguing, man!" Jasmine said.

"All right, pet, all right," Neil said. "We're just glad you're home is all."

"I just wanna get to bed."

"Aye, you get yourself up to bed. But lookit, I'm gonna come up in five, all right? We're just gonna have a quick talk. About Daniel Moore. That's the lad what done it, but we can't find him. So if –"

"Dad, man!"

"Neil, man!"

Someone hurried up the stairs. They almost slipped a couple of times and Graeme guessed it was Jasmine. Another set of footsteps followed her up, probably Lydia, then he heard Neil talk to Michael. He sighed. "I'm gonna have to gan straighten this out. You sort the lads, ring round and see if anyone's seen or heard anything."

"All right," Michael said.

Neil went upstairs.

Graeme waved Tony to him. "Howay."

Tony followed. "Where we going?"

They caught Michael in the hallway, halfway through a door.

"We're going out, Mike," Graeme said.

Michael paused, half-turned. "Where?"

"Gonna check in on Carl, see if there's owt else he can tell us. Unless you've got something else in mind?"

"Nah. Fine. Can't hurt. The little wanker says anything worthwhile, just give us a bell."

***

They drove to Fenham in silence. Pulling to the kerb outside the house, Graeme turned to Tony. "I've huffed you."

"Huffed? I'm not a bairn, Graeme."

"You're acting like one."

"You've pissed us off."

"Lookit, you might be under the impression that I was a bit coy with the details at first, but I've been very open with you since. And I was fuckin right, wasn't I?"

"Right about what?"

"Brought in on one job, then getting dragged into the rest of it."

"Suppose you were. But you're the one that's dragged us along, mate. And I'm still pissed off."

"What else you got going on?"

"I've got a fucking job, man, Graeme! I don't work for Neil Doyle, this isn't all expenses paid for me! I've still gotta pay me rent and bills, man. That fucker's costing us me wages again!"

"Divvint worry about that. I'll sort that out."

"Oh, aye? What with? Didn't realise you were sitting on a pot of gold."

"I'll talk to Neil. Once this is sorted, he'll be in a better mood. He'll reimburse you for this. He'll appreciate you for helping out. He's got a good memory for loyalty, has Neil."

"Here man, why're you always talking to me like I'm after an in with Neil Doyle? I'm not. I'm more than fuckin happy being on the outside."

"It never hurts to have friends, Tony."

"They're not the kind of friends I wanna have."

"Here, ring up the club you're working, tell them you're gonna miss a few shifts –"

"A *few* shifts?"

"Tell them you don't know how many exactly, say it might just be the one, might be a couple more – and tell them you're helping out Neil Doyle. They won't hassle you. You see how important it is to have friends then, when no one's hassling you cos you've missed work."

Tony looked out the window, shook his head.

"Howay," Graeme said. "Let's go see him."

They didn't bother to knock. They were ready to kick the door open but it was already unlocked, same as last time. Graeme wondered if they ever bothered to lock it at all. They went straight up to Carl's room. He was home. He'd had his fingers bound, and his right hand was held close to his ribs while he sat at his desk and attempted to roll a cigarette one-handed. There was an open suitcase on his bed, the unfolded clothes stuffed haphazardly inside. He jumped up when Graeme and Tony entered his room, dropped the half-wrapped cigarette and held out his good hand.

"Calm down, son," Graeme said. "You don't have to go anywhere today." He made a point of looking at the suitcase. "Though it looks like you're planning a trip."

"Aye, well." Carl swallowed. "Figured it might be a good idea if I'm not round for a while."

"Going back down to Boro?"

"Boro? Fuck no."

"Don't reckon your parents would be too impressed if you turned up with your hand how it is."

"My parents?" He laughed and shook his head. "Richie's got a bit of a motor mouth on him, hasn't he? Who fucking knew? Anything he *didn't* tell yous?"

"He didn't tell us who stuck the dart in Jasmine's eye. And he didn't tell us where Daniel is."

Carl shrugged. "If he wasn't at home, there's

nothing I can do to help. He lives with his dad. If one of them's not there the other tends to be. Ask his dad. I'm sure he'd be glad to assist. Ask him really nice and he might tell you."

"We've asked."

"Oh."

"Nowhere else?"

"I don't know."

Graeme sighed. "You're starting to piss us off, son."

"Would you rather I just lied, send you on a wild goose chase?"

"I'd rather you thought about it really hard."

Carl shrugged. "Well, there's his lass."

"They ran off together that night."

"Someone was paying attention! Aye, they ran off together, but he's not gonna be hiding there, is he? I mean, that's the first place anyone would have looked, isn't it?" He grinned.

"Y'kna what, son? There it is. You've pissed me off. Has he pissed you off, Tony?"

"He's a cocky little cunt," Tony said.

"Have a look at his fingers, will you, Tony?"

Tony crossed the room, grabbed Carl by the wrist with one hand and wrapped the other round his bound fingers. Carl cried out. "No, no, *wait* – hold on, hold on!"

"Got some ideas?"

Carl's eyes darted side to side, then they lit up. "His uncle!"

"His uncle?"

"You know his uncle, aye? Paddy Moore?"

"I know him."

"Fucking nutter, isn't he?"

"What about him, Carl?"

"Just let go of us, all right?" Carl was pleading. He looked as pathetic as he sounded. Tony let go, gave him a little shove. Carl almost lost his balance, managed to steady himself against the desk. Tony stayed close. Carl cleared his throat. "He might have gone there. To his uncle's."

"Paddy stays mobile, from what I heard."

"Aye, he's a paranoid motherfucker. But he does have a pad. Like, a regular place. A *home*, almost. It's in Byker. No one knows about it. Me and Carl went there a couple of times, got high. I hated it. Paddy, man – he just stares you out. He's one of those psychos you never know if he's just gonna stare the whole time or if he's gonna snap over some imagined slight and start slapping you all over."

"Aye, sounds like Paddy."

"I only went like twice, but Dan might've gone there. Family, aye?"

"You reckon he's still got the place?"

"I don't know for definite, but it's worth a look, right?" Carl sounded like he was imploring them, desperate for his information to be worth something.

"Got an address?"

"Yeah."

"Write it down, son."

5

Patrick Moore was a recluse. Whenever possible he kept away from people, and only had anything to do with them when it suited his own needs.

He was also a violent, ill-tempered, highly dangerous man. His name inspired dread in all who knew him. Though his specific skill set was often in demand, he didn't do anything that wasn't on his own terms. Few people would go directly to him when looking to recruit for a score, it was said not even his own brother. If Patrick was looking for work, he let it be known.

Likewise, if ever the mood for violence fell upon him, as it often did, he would head out of his own accord and find someone to hurt. He never looked for long. He wasn't fussy who he fought.

But most of the time he remained committed to his hermitic lifestyle, stayed locked away, alone. He'd disappear for long stretches, then resurface just as abruptly. No one knew where he went. No one knew where he lived, and he went to great lengths to keep it that way. It was rumoured, and widely believed, that he kept secret pads all over the north east, some of them furnished with nothing more than a mattress and a television.

Tony drove, Graeme sat in the passenger seat. They followed Michael's car, passing under streetlights that led the way to Byker like an airport landing strip. There were a couple of skinheads riding with Michael. If Patrick was in, they were prepared for trouble.

"You think he's gonna be here?" Tony said.

"Which one?"

"The kid."

"Hopefully. Get this over with."

"And if he's not?"

Graeme blew air. "Then we'll get ourselves on another fuckin goose chase and see what we can shake loose."

"When's it end?"

"When it's done."

Tony blew air. "Aye." He sat in silence while stopped for a traffic light, then took a left turn, stuck on Michael. "What're we doing here? They don't need us."

"Not everyone's been invited. Feel honoured."

"There you go again, saying things I should feel but don't."

"I was being facetious, man."

"Uh-huh. You had anything to do with this fella?"

"Paddy? Couple of run-ins."

"What's he like?"

"Like Carl said – he's a fucking nutter."

"Had trouble?"

Graeme looked out the window, at the buildings that lined the road. It was late and there weren't many people on the streets, but those that were blurred on the pavements as they drove past. "If you go to see Paddy, you best be ready for a fight."

"You got a story to go with that cryptic warning?"

"I've got a few. But all right, here's one. First time I met him. He's younger than me, obviously, but back when I was still pretty young myself and he was first starting out I got a call from a friend was having some trouble with him.

He ripped him off. Paddy Moore's always been a troublesome prick, ever since he was a kid from what I've heard. Always in a scrap. You get some kids like that, don't ya? Little animals, and unless you get them caged early enough, they stay that way. Paddy's stayed that way."

"That's a nice way of putting it, Graeme. Get to the point, man."

"Here, I'll tell it me own way. You asked for a story. Y'kna, when you were younger, you didn't complain about how I told a tale."

"That was then, and I had a lot more time and patience. I wanted all the details cos I could tell me friends about it, impress them that me mam was with this hard bloke from the city. But these days I'm living the same life you are, and I like people to get to the meat of the thing when they're telling us a story."

"Oh aye, I see how it is. But I'll tell you one thing, son – you're not living the same life I am."

"We're in the same world now, Graeme."

"Look man, we're getting off topic. I thought you wanted the meat of the thing."

"Why aye, man. Get to it."

"Right. So. Anyway, Paddy was starting out and me mate saw some promise in him, thought it would be a good idea to have a strongman psycho by his side, so he goes into business with him. Pills, mainly, that was their thing. Paddy took the pills, sold them on, kept the profit. Told me mate to go and fuck himself.

"The lad was a bit of a wimp, like. That's why he was impressed by the strong-arm type, but he knew he couldn't get Paddy telt himself. He asked me to go talk to him. Said he was willing to take half of the profit, but, y'kna, there's me being Billy-big-balls, said I'd get it all back. Anyway, I went to Paddy's, introduced meself, he let me in, all nicey-nicey. So nice, in fact, there's me thinking I was actually intimidating the cunt, that he might just give us the cash and that'd be that. Such a nice guy I was thinking fuck it, I'd just ask for the half, like me pal said.

"Then he turned. Still nicey-nicey, but he was different, y'kna? Cold. Smiled with all his teeth. Asked why I was there. I told him. He just stared at us, with that smile, then he belted us all over his front fucking room and kicked us out the house. He was like a fucking whirlwind, man."

"So he kicked you in?"

"Aye."

"He done it since?"

"I learnt me lesson after that. We've been round each other a few times since, but I don't stay with him long, and I don't go alone. He hasn't mellowed with age. Remember what I said about animals? You get these rescue dogs, some of them have been bred for fighting. They get taken when their handlers are arrested, they go to pens, for the first time in their lives they're shown some care and affection. It gets so you can stroke them without them snapping for your hand. But you've always got that fear around them, haven't you? You never leave them alone with kids. You're always waiting, always prepared, for when they try to take a bite out of you. That's Paddy. And he's got some sharp fucking teeth."

"So how d'you think they're gonna muzzle him?"

"Whey, I doubt they're gonna knock and ask politely if young Daniel has been sleeping over. Reckon it's gonna be a case of smash and grab. Saying that, I reckon if anyone has a decent chance against the cunt one on one, it'd be Michael."

Michael's car pulled down a back alley, killed its lights then came to a gradual stop. Tony did the same. Michael and the two with him got out. Graeme wound down his window as they approached.

"It's that one on the end," Michael said. He pointed. "According to your little pal, anyway." The house was at the bottom of the alley. The windows were in darkness.

"Doesn't look like anyone's home," Graeme said.

"We'll see. These two are going round the front, I'm taking the back. They try to leg it, that's the way they're gonna go. They get past me, you two collar them. Got it?" He looked at Graeme, then Tony.

"Got it," Tony said.

"Good. They *do* get past, Daniel's your priority. Get him pinned down. Leave Paddy to me."

"Gladly," Graeme said.

Michael and his two skinheads went down the alley, to the house. Graeme and Tony got out the car, followed them halfway then hung back. It was the kind of back alley where once upon a time washing lines would have hung from wall to wall, strung with fluttering bed sheets that would have made passing through on foot difficult, and in a car impossible. Kids would have jumped screaming from the roofs of the outhouses and sheds, chasing each other through the makeshift clothes-tunnels. Now there was broken glass in the gutters and swastikas sprayed on the walls. The clotheslines had all been cut down, long ago.

At the end of the alley they could see Michael. They watched as he carefully, quietly opened the gate, took up position near the back door. The top half of the door was frosted glass. The hallway beyond was dark. The two skinheads went round the front. Graeme listened for their knock. He watched the house. Michael stood to the side of the door, away from the glass. The knock came. Three hard, policeman-style raps that echoed through the night. Graeme thought they probably should have knocked softer, been less obvious.

Michael's fists opened and closed. His shoulders were hunched. He was ready for battle. Beside him, Graeme could hear Tony's breath, short, sharp, expectant intakes. Whether he realised it or not, he was bouncing on the balls of his feet, like a boxer preparing for a fight.

Upstairs, the curtains were drawn. One of them twitched. Graeme looked to the back door. A light had come on. Michael stayed where he was. A shadow appeared at the glass. Michael braced. The shadow stayed where it was. Graeme heard something called, too muffled for him to make out. Michael stepped in front of the glass. "Just come on out and we'll —"

An explosion took his words. Glass shattered. Graeme grabbed Tony's arm and they threw themselves to the ground. Graeme looked back to see Michael hit the floor like a felled tree. Through the shattered window he saw Paddy flee, hit the light, cast the hallway in darkness again. Upstairs, the curtain was still. Inside the house, he heard something shouted, again unintelligible. Michael lay very still on the ground. Graeme and Tony ran to him. The two skinheads came skidding down the side of the house. Graeme heard a door open and close, heard footsteps at the front racing away, quickly fade into silence. He thought to tell the skinheads to get round there, to go after them, but then he looked at Michael. The shotgun blast had caught him in the chest, torn it up, and shards of glass had ricocheted and embedded into his face and neck too. He was bleeding heavily. The four gathered around him didn't know what to do. Graeme looked at the others, but everyone else seemed to be looking at him. All he could do was watch Michael bleed.

He was still breathing. The breaths were ragged, though, and there was a gargling sound at the back of his throat. His eyes were open, but blinking. They were looking upwards, to the stars.

6

Two weeks passed. Graeme returned to his flat, laid low and waited for a phone call. Tony went back to work.

Michael was on an intensive care unit, in a coma. There were tubes running in and out seemingly every inch of him. Graeme hadn't been to see him, but he'd been told. That night in Byker, watching him bleed out, he'd thought that was the end for the lad. Thought he was watching him die. Someone, he didn't know who, called an ambulance. Probably the same skinhead that had balls big enough to call Neil, tell him what had happened. Neil was surprisingly calm. Well, maybe not calm, but he still had his head about him enough to give out orders – he told the skinheads to stay there, and for Graeme and Tony to make themselves scarce before the police turned up. They hadn't needed told twice.

Graeme was in Shannon's café, sipping on coffee, when the inevitable call finally came. He hadn't eaten anything. He'd barely eaten since the night Michael got shot. When he looked at himself in the mornings, he actually thought he'd lost some weight. His gut was looking trimmer, his face was thinner too, but his beard was thicker and his hair was longer. He put it down to nerves, the lack of care he was taking of himself. He knew something was coming, something bad. It wasn't over yet. There would be repercussions. They were going to be bloody. It had gone beyond Jasmine's eye. It was a borderline war.

"You all right, Graeme?" Shannon leaned over the counter to speak to him.

"Eh? Oh, I'm not bad, pet."

"You don't look very well, love."

"Just a bit peaky."

"Been peaky a while now, haven't you?"

Graeme shrugged, took a drink. The coffee had gone cold.

"You still not sleeping too well?"

"Not really."

"Doesn't look like you're eating, either. I can't get you something?"

"Nah pet, I'm all right."

"What about –"

His phone started to ring. He pulled it out, gave Shannon an apologetic look and said a quick goodbye, then took the call outside. It was an unrecognised number, but he had a feeling he knew who it was. "Hello?"

"Lookit, it's Neil – just listen. Get yourself to the Baltic, the café there, I'll be along in an hour. Bring Tony."

Before Graeme could respond, Neil had hung up. He put the phone away, put his hands deep in his pockets and watched his breath cloud before his face. All of a sudden he felt hungry.

***

Tony did not come without protest, but he did come.

"Why should I give a shit about his steroid-pumped son, or his slutty daughter? First time I had a run-in with her, she kicks off to daddy dearest and I've gotta waste my time on a straightener, where her big, *big* fucking brother nearly knocks me teeth down me throat. And I've gotta waste my time on *this*. I mean, when I thought we were just picking up some kid, fine, a five minute job, but now people are getting stabbed, fucking shotguns are going off – howay, man! When's enough enough?"

"All right. But Michael just slapped you round a bit. Aye he broke your nose, but he's in a coma now, could be he's gonna vegetate the rest of his life – it's hardly a fair punishment, is it?" They walked along the Quayside, crossed the Millennium Bridge onto the Gateshead side of the Tyne. The sun was shining, but it was cold. There were people milling up and down the path next to the river, mostly on the Newcastle side, and most of them looked like students. Some of them, the ones that were not from the area, either overseas or from the south, took pictures of themselves with their mobile phones with the iconic bridges in the background.

"That what you think? Where does *fair* come into it? Doyle's planning on plucking out a lad's eye because he *accidentally* blinded his daughter, and you're talking about *fair*?" They entered the Baltic and took the elevator up to the café. Graeme knew Neil would be waiting there already. He wasn't the type to take his time and appreciate the current art installations elsewhere in the building.

"That's enough of that now, right? We divvint want him to hear."

"Right." Tony looked out the window on the way up, at the sunlight glistening on the surface of the Tyne. "We don't want Neil fucking Doyle to hear anything we have to say."

Neil had a table by the window, but he wasn't enjoying the view. He'd been clearly watching for their entrance, waved them over as soon as the elevator doors opened. He was alone. "Take a seat, hurry up," he said. "We haven't got long."

Graeme and Tony sat. "You all right, then?" Graeme said.

Neil got straight to business. "Here's the crack – fuckin police are all over the house, I've had to sneak out. I've got maybe five minutes left here then I've gotta get back, so just *listen*. Paddy hasn't gone to ground, not entirely. He's been seen in Walker. Hangs out in a pub, same one every day, called the Dog and Bone. No one knows where he's staying, though, probably one of those pads he seems to have stashed away all over the fuckin place. Get yourselves over there, and get him. Am I clear?"

Graeme sucked his teeth. "It's not like him to just be *seen*, especially not every day. You divvint reckon he's setting us up for something here?"

"Maybe he is. You lads be extra careful then, eh?"

Graeme cleared his throat, saw that Neil was eager to leave and had no interest in discussing things further. "Aye."

"Right." Neil got to his feet. "Quick as you can then, eh?"

***

The Dog and Bone was a pit, a poorly lit hovel more akin to a cave than a pub. The men drinking in it looked like they drank there every day, and they raised their heads and their eyebrows when Graeme and Tony, two strangers, entered. Paddy was not present, but they had counted on this. They'd watched the front for a while first before they entered, they'd seen everyone who'd gone inside.

Tony took a table in the corner behind the door. They'd have a clear view of anyone coming in, but they wouldn't be seen themselves. They had to get a good look at Paddy, make sure it was him and that they weren't just wasting their time. Graeme ordered a couple of pints from the battleaxe behind the counter. She seemed to have one facial expression, and it was immensely displeased. She said nothing, other than to demand payment, and to grunt at Graeme's thanks.

"It's all making sense now," Tony said when he brought the drinks.

"What's that?" They spoke in hushed tones so no one could hear, though it didn't seem like anyone had any interest in them now they were out of sight.

"The night Michael got shot, when Doyle told us to leg it before the police got there. It's so he still had us out here, so he still had someone on the outside that he could send about doing his dirty work."

Graeme didn't drink his beer. The glass was filthy, and the liquid itself had a filmy surface. "Neil does consider all the angles."

"Takes a callous man to consider all the angles when it looks like his son – his *only* son – is about to bleed to fucking death."

"Mm."

"And I'll tell you another thing, an'all. Back there at the Baltic, he didn't mention Michael *once*. You fucking believe that? It was like nothing had happened. Like the lad's not lying in a hospital bed with a machine doing all his breathing for him."

"What do you want us to say, Tony?"

"I don't know, man. I just wanna see or hear something from you so I know you've got some fucking thoughts in your head beyond blindly following this arsehole."

Graeme said nothing. He watched the door. Tony picked up his drink, raised it to his mouth and almost took a mouthful of it. He held it up to the faint light then curled his lip and put it back down.

"So what do you think?" Tony said. "Think this is a set up?"

"I think Paddy wants to be seen. He's not scared of Doyle – shit man, he's not scared of anyone. And he knows that the only way Daniel can be safe of Doyle, is if Doyle's…well, if he's dead. I reckon Paddy would quite happily set up fort somewhere round here and take out everyone that gets sent after him until there's no one left. He's a fucking nutter, but tactically he's sound. He knows what he's doing. He'll take Doyle out guerrilla style, just take out everyone that comes his way until there's no one left."

"Like with Michael."

"Exactly."

"And we're the poor mugs that've been lined up next."

The thought almost made Graeme want to take a drink of the filthy beer. "Aye."

They sat for an hour before Paddy arrived. He said his hello's to a couple of people, conversed with the bartender. He was all smiles, seemed to be in a good mood. At the sight of him, Graeme felt his stomach dip and flutter, felt all the memories and fears resurface. He remembered being beaten round Paddy's front room, punched and kicked and thrown until he was seeing stars and beginning to genuinely fear for his life. His mouth went dry and he set his jaw, tried to hide his growing panic so Tony wouldn't notice. He tapped Tony on the arm and they slid out, went to the car. They'd parked it at the kerb on the other side of the street. They watched the front door, waited for him to leave.

***

It was dark by the time Paddy left. Tony had fallen asleep. Graeme hit him awake and they got out the car, followed on foot, made sure they kept their distance. He led them to a precinct made up of two charity shops, a newsagent's, and a cafe. It was late and they were all closed. Paddy's flat was above one of the charity shops. Tony stayed and kept an eye on the lights, made sure Paddy didn't leave again, while Graeme hurried back and got the car in case they needed to make a hasty retreat.

"How we gonna do this?" Tony said.

Graeme went to the back of the car. "You saw how it went when they tried to play it sneaky." He opened the boot.

"Kick the door down?"

"We're not gonna talk to him. He seem like the kind wants to talk? We're not gonna waste our breath." Graeme reached into the boot, pulled out a hammer. He pushed the handle up his sleeve so it was concealed, then gripped it tightly by the neck, the cold metal of the head bringing an ache to his knuckles. "Catch him by surprise. And if we're lucky, the young'un will be here an'all."

"You think anything ever surprises a motherfucker *that* edgy?"

"Probably not. Sometimes paranoia is your best defence. But if we're *extra* lucky, we'll get him before he gets the shotgun."

"That supposed to be funny?"

"No."

They went round the back of the precinct, up the steps that led to the flats. The door had no windows, but there was a spy-hole. Light shone through it. Graeme and Tony exchanged glances. Graeme squeezed the hammer's handle. Tony popped his knuckles. The door didn't have a handle, just a keyhole. Graeme gave it a push. It was locked. He wasn't surprised. They looked at each other again. Graeme stepped back, braced himself. He eyed up the door, then raised a leg and kicked hard, threw everything he had into it.

The door rocked in its frame, but it didn't break open. "*Fuck*!" He tried again. The door stayed firm.

"Howay man, Graeme," Tony said. "Fuckin *kick* it!"

Graeme shot Tony a look, then threw his shoulder into the door, beginning to feel ridiculous. Tony pushed him aside, raised his own boot. Graeme heard steps on the other side. He pushed Tony down then threw himself the other way. An explosion tore through the door from the other side. Graeme felt splinters rain down around him. His ears rang. He turned, saw Tony scrambling to his feet.

The door opened. Paddy stepped out. He was barefoot, wore jeans and a vest. The shotgun was still smoking. He swung it toward Tony. Graeme lunged at his feet, smashed his toes with the hammer. Paddy screamed, loosed the other barrel. It went into the air, but Tony dived aside anyway. The two crushed toes on Paddy's right foot left a bloody smear on the ground as he stumbled back. Graeme tackled him, drove him into the flat, down the hallway. He heard the shotgun fall behind him. He drove Paddy into the front room, they went over the sofa. Graeme clutched the hammer, held onto it for dear life. Paddy landed on top, pinned him with his knees. His face was bright red, and he was laughing. Graeme thought of his brother, of Robert strapped to the chair. They had the same laugh.

The first punch caught Graeme in the cheek. His head spun, barely had time to settle before the next punch landed in his eye. He worked his arm loose, swung the hammer. Paddy laughed harder, grabbed Graeme's wrist, bit his fingers and prised the weapon from his hand. He pinned the arm again, raised the hammer.

Tony tackled him, then rolled through and jumped to his feet. Paddy was slowed by his mangled foot, but he got up and the two exchanged punches. He was no less ferocious — if anything, the pain made him madder. His blows rocked Tony, almost knocked him down. Tony ducked, parried, managed to bloody Paddy's mouth. In return, Paddy hooked him across the jaw. Tony's legs buckled, he dropped to his knees. Paddy punched him square in the face, sent him back.

Graeme rolled onto his side. Paddy saw him move, kicked him hard in the ribs with his bad foot. He roared as he did it, blood poured from his ruined toes, but the pain spurred him on and he kicked Graeme over and over. Graeme coughed, the breath driven from him, his ribs feeling like they were cracking, about to break, then finally the kicking stopped and Paddy dropped to his arse, held his foot in both hands and squeezed it, his teeth grit. The veins popped in his neck. He groaned, but it sounded more like a growl. Graeme coughed again. He could taste blood.

Paddy pushed himself across the floor until his back was to the wall. He braced against it and used it for support as he stood. Tony had started to rise. His nose was bleeding and he kept shaking his head, like his vision and balance were all shot. Paddy went to him, grabbed his head in both hands, then brought his knee up into his face. He didn't let go. He did it again. He alternated knees.

Graeme crawled across the floor, to the hammer. He reached it, wrapped his hand around it. It was hard to get up. He put an arm across his aching ribs, went to the wall like Paddy had and used it. When he turned, Tony was limp, his face bloodied. Graeme struck Paddy across the back of the head with the hammer. There was a dull thud. Paddy let go of Tony as he toppled forward. Graeme dropped to his knees, followed him to the ground. He rolled Paddy onto his back. Tony coughed, still conscious. He wiped blood from his eyes and propped himself up on an elbow.

Paddy's eyes were glazed. He started to blink repeatedly like he was having some kind of fit. When he stopped, his eyes rolled round in his skull. They settled on Graeme. He grinned. There was blood on his teeth. He clawed at Graeme's face, just managed to catch him on the chin. He grabbed for Graeme's throat with both hands, squeezed, but the hammer blow had weakened him, sapped his strength.

Graeme brought the hammer across his face, knocked his teeth loose, sent them skidding across the floor. Paddy let go of his neck. Graeme held his shoulder, pinned him, struck him again. The hammer landed in the centre of his forehead, burst the flesh there, cracked the bone. Graeme hit him again, hit him over and over until Paddy's legs jerked in his death throes and finally he was still. Blood and skull spattered the floor and the walls, the front of Graeme's clothes and his face. The contents of Paddy's head oozed across the ground.

Graeme fell back, panting. He dropped the hammer.

Tony wiped more blood from his eyes, cleared his throat then had a coughing fit. When it ended, he said "I think Neil wanted him alive."

Graeme wheezed. It took him a long time to catch his breath. He slid across the floor and put his back against the sofa. There was a mobile phone on the arm. He slid it into his own pocket. "If Neil wanted him alive, then Neil could bloody well come here and get him himself," he said.

"If he can sneak out the house, past the coppers, he can get himself over here and sort his own fucking dirty work. But he didn't. So right now I don't give a shit what Neil wants."

Tony laughed. "There it is. That's what I wanted to hear."

"Eh?"

"*He can sort his own fucking dirty work*. That's what you said. That's what I needed to hear from you Graeme. I was getting worried."

"Worried about what? I don't know what you're goin on about, son."

"Course you do. And here, listen." Tony put a finger in the air. "You hear that?"

"No sirens."

"Aye. No coppers." Tony got to his feet. It took a long time. His face was entirely red and swollen. He leaned against the wall for support. He peered out a window from around a curtain. "Nowt," he said. "How rough's this fucking place that no one calls the police when there's a fucking shotgun going off?"

Graeme looked at the dead body in the centre of the room, the face smashed beyond all recognition. He could feel it still, the impact running up and down his arm. "No one wants to know," he said. "They don't want any fucking part of it. And I divvint fucking blame them."

7

One of the skinheads snuck them in the back door. A police car was still parked out front. Neil gave them both the once over. "You look like shit."

Neither said anything. Tony rubbed his swollen jaw.

"You clean up your mess?"

"Course we did," Graeme said.

"Good. So what happened?"

"He nearly killed us."

"And?"

"He didn't."

"He's dead."

"Aye."

"Y'kna, I wanna be pissed off, but I'm almost impressed."

Graeme and Tony looked at each other.

"And the lad wasn't there," Neil said.

"No."

"You didn't think to maybe enquire as to his whereabouts before you did Paddy in?"

"Come on – you know Paddy was never gonna say a word."

"So what'd you get?"

"Beaten up."

Neil blew air through his nose.

"How's Michael?"

"What's that supposed to mean?"

"It's not supposed to mean anything. How is he?"

Neil rubbed his eyes, sighed. "No change. But he's fit, and he's strong, and he'll pull through."

"The doctors said that?"

"You know what doctors are like, they won't commit to anything. But I know it. He's my boy, and he'll pull through. In the meantime, they've just gotta do their job and keep a close eye on him. And I fucking told them, it better be a *close* fucking eye." Neil crossed his arms, bit his lip, looked like he was thinking. "Right. So. This kid, Daniel. His dad's dead, his uncle's dead – he's ran out of family and he's all out of friends. There's no one left to protect him, but there's no one left that can tell us where he is."

Graeme didn't mention the phone. Neil would jump straight on it, find Daniel's number and shout threats down the line. It wouldn't accomplish anything.

"So I hope you've got a fucking idea what to do next."

"We need to talk to Jasmine."

Neil gave him a sidelong glance, raised an eyebrow.

"Daniel's got a girlfriend. Carl mentioned her."

"Ask Carl."

"Carl's gone."

"You let him go?"

"We didn't let him do anything, but he's gone."

"Then ask Richie."

"I'm already here."

"What good's the girlfriend?"

"Either she's gone with him, or maybe she has an idea where it is he's at."

Neil eyed them both. Graeme eyed him back. Tony reclined on the sofa, probed at his various cuts and bruises.

"Howay then. She's in her room. Lydia's in with her, mind. She's not gonna like it. I've tried since the young'un got home, Lydia won't let me ask her nowt."

Tony seemed willing to stay behind with a finger in his mouth, inspecting his chipped teeth, but Graeme dragged him out the seat. They followed Neil up the stairs, along the hall to Jasmine's room. They waited outside while Neil went in. Voices were raised, Lydia's particularly. They were muffled by the door, but there was no mistaking her angry *no*'s. Neil's voice began to rise. The back and forth shouting went on for a couple of minutes, then Lydia stormed out. She stomped down the hallway to another room, slammed the door behind her. Graeme and Tony looked at each other. Tony raised his eyebrows. Neil followed Lydia out, spoke to Graeme. "Two minutes," he said, then went after his wife.

Graeme and Tony went in. Jasmine sat cross-legged on her bed. She wore a turquoise dressing gown wrapped tightly round her, leopard print pyjama pants and fluffy bunny slippers. Her hair, unwashed, was piled into a bun atop her head. Her face, devoid of its usual layers of make-up, looked pale and unwell, had acquired a smattering of spots upon her cheeks and chin. She looked at them with her one eye. The patch was jarring.

"Hello, pet," Graeme said.

Jasmine nodded.

He spoke to her gently, but he tried not to be patronising. More than a fortnight had passed since they'd witnessed her return home, and though Graeme doubted she had left her room since then, there'd been enough time for her to grow accustomed to her disability. Speaking to her like a child wasn't going to benefit him in any way. "You know why we're here, don't you?"

She shrugged. "I can probably guess."

"Anything you can tell us, then?"

She shrugged again.

"It's a big favour, pet, but y'kna what your dad's like. We don't get this sorted out shortly, he's not gonna be best pleased with us. So anything you can give us, it's gonna be a big hand. We need to find him."

Jasmine looked past Graeme, to Tony. "I recognise you," she said.

Tony snorted.

"Dan has a girlfriend, doesn't he, Jasmine?" Graeme said. "Charlotte? That right?"

"Michael beat you up pretty badly, didn't he?" She'd ignored Graeme, was still talking to Tony.

Tony shifted his weight from one foot to the other. "Aye."

"That was a few months ago now, wasn't it? Looks like someone else has beat you up since."

"It's getting to be a habit. Must be the company I keep." He looked at Graeme.

"What're you doing here?"

"I keep asking myself the same thing."

"It's not for me. You wouldn't do anything for me, not after I grassed you up. You don't care that Michael's been shot, because he beat you up. Broke your nose, didn't he? It looked like he did. I don't think you like any of us very much, not after what we did to you. It must be for the money, right?"

"I'm not getting paid."

"Then what's the crack? You just as loyal as this one?" She tilted her head toward Graeme.

"I guess I'm loyal to someone." A scab had opened on his cheek, a single line of blood ran down his face. He used a finger to wipe it away. "Not necessarily your dad."

"Where's Charlotte live, Jasmine?" Graeme said.

She finally turned back to Graeme. "What difference does it make?"

"You know why we need to see her."

"He didn't do it on purpose."

"It's too late for that."

"He's my friend."

"Your dad doesn't care."

Jasmine rubbed her good eye. "I don't want him to get hurt. Daniel...I know about his dad, and his uncle, I know they're a couple of hard cases, but Daniel's not like them." She rubbed her eye harder. "When I was in hospital, right after it happened, I was angry, and I wanted him hurt, and I wanted to claw his eyes out myself – but I'm not angry anymore. It wasn't his fault. He doesn't deserve this." She let her hand drop. The white of her eye, and the skin around it, was red.

"You told your dad?"

"He won't listen."

"Because you're his little girl, and someone's hurt you."

"And now his son, my brother, has been hurt because of it."

"You know there's only one way this is gonna end. It's not with you, or me, or anyone whose name isn't Neil Doyle getting what they want."

"I know." She turned to Tony again. "You got a girlfriend?"

Tony sucked his teeth. "Not at the minute."

"You're not bad lookin, when your face isn't all messed up."

"Thanks."

"What about me?"

"What about you?"

"Before you had the straightener with Michael,

before you kicked us out the club, back when I wasn't a fuckin Cyclops, if you saw me walkin down the street, what would you think? Without knowin us, what would you think?"

"I dunno."

"I'm not your type."

"I don't have a type."

"Then what?"

"I dunno."

Graeme shot him a narrow-eyed look that he hoped conveyed the message, *Throw the lass a fuckin bone, man.*

"Well. Y'kna. You were all right."

"All right?"

"Aye. All right."

"What do you think now?"

"I think you look tired, pet."

"Aye. I don't look in the mirror much, cos I get hung up on this." She pointed at her missing eye. "I just get depressed with it. But whenever I do catch a glimpse of meself, I look fuckin rough." She stared into a corner of the room, away from the two men, fingered a growing spot on her jaw, squeezed the edges of it though it had no head. "Before it happened, before I got stuck with that bloody dart, there was this lad I was kind of seeing. We'd met up a couple of times, we were texting a lot. I got a text off him the morning after, when I was in the hospital, just a response to whatever it was I'd said to him last. I messaged him back, told him I was in the hospital, but that was it. Didn't give any details or anything. I expected, I guess I kind of hoped, he'd ask some questions, y'kna? Show some concern. Try to come see me. Well, I don't know what he's heard, but he hasn't messaged us since." She shrugged. "News travels, doesn't it? He'll know. He'll know I've lost the eye. And now he's lost all interest."

Graeme shot Tony another look, urged him to say something positive. Jasmine wasn't looking at them. Tony rolled his eyes.

"Well, if that kind of thing matters to him, he sounds like a prick anyway, aye?"

Graeme prompted him to say more. Tony pulled a face.

"So you're better off without. I mean, lookit, it's just an eye, you're still the same person. You really care if someone that shallow stops messaging you over it? Once you get through this, y'kna, this initial hump, you'll do yourself back up, show him what he's missing out on. Then he'll feel like a right mug, won't he? You can get yourself one of them fancy eye patches, the kind that's all bejewelled."

Graeme stared at him again, wide-eyed, concerned he was going too far, but then he heard Jasmine giggle, looked at her and saw she was smiling.

"Aye, that's what I'll do. I'll get meself a fancy eye patch." She laughed. "Every night will be pirate night. Reckon I could pull off sexy pirate?"

"I'm sure if anyone can, it'll be you."

She smiled at Tony, and Tony forced one back at her.

Graeme gave them a moment, waited until Jasmine turned away again. "Where does Charlotte live, pet?" he said.

Jasmine held her breath. With her one red eye she looked at Graeme, then Tony, then back at Graeme. "All right," she said. "Just get it over with."

8

Charlotte lived in Newcastle, the downstairs flat of a converted house. She was home when they knocked. She opened the door tentatively, seemed to instinctively know who they were. Probably the wounds on their faces gave them away as heavies. Her shoulders sagged.

"Can we come in, pet?" Graeme said.

"All right." Her voice was very quiet. She backed into the room as they entered, watched them. Tony closed the door. Charlotte's shoulders bunched back up, the tension she'd no doubt felt for the past couple of weeks returning to her now the two men were inside her home. Her fists were closed, but not defensively. She was trying to hide the way she shook.

Graeme took in the room, looked her over. It smelled like Chinese takeaway and wine. There was a half-empty bottle of red and a stained glass on the floor next to the sofa, where there lay a bunched up blanket and a couple of bed pillows. Charlotte wore sweatpants and thick socks, a jumper with holes in the front and in the sleeves.

Graeme turned to Tony. "Check the rooms."

"He-he's not here," Charlotte said.

"I don't reckon he is, pet," Graeme said. "But we'd better check, eh? Take a seat."

Charlotte walked backward to the sofa, which appeared as if it was doubling as her makeshift bed. She sat down, pushed the blanket to one side. The television was on, but it was muted. She grabbed the remote and turned it off.

There was a chair opposite the sofa. Graeme sat on it, groaned as he took the weight off his feet. Tony returned. "Not here," he said.

"Aye." Graeme tapped his fingers on the arm of the chair. He watched Charlotte. She squirmed under his gaze. Beyond her there was a bookshelf. One shelf was half-full with books, the rest held ornaments and framed photographs. The light was dim, only a lamp on a table next to the sofa switched on, but Graeme could make out the family in one of them. The parents, a younger Charlotte and her younger sister. The picture next to it was a more up to date image of Charlotte, her arms around a young man. Graeme guessed it was Daniel. They were both smiling, laughing, messing about for the camera.

"I don't know where he is," she said, the words tumbling out of her mouth.

Graeme nodded. "All right."

"I've tried ringing him, and texting him, but he won't respond. His phone's on, every time I call it's on, it rings, but he doesn't answer, and he won't call me back. I've left him voice messages, but I don't know if he even listens to them."

"When'd you last see him?"

"That night, when it happened. We ran off together, I had his hand, I thought we were going to come here but then he just stopped, let go of me. He was trying to talk, but he couldn't. I was going to follow him but he just kept pushing me away, then finally he started swearing, saying something about how I couldn't go with him, telling me to go – but I wouldn't, so he ran off."

"Where'd he go?"

"I don't know."

"You stopped following him?"

"I tried, but he kept swearing, and he was faster than me. I went to his place, but he wasn't there."

"You look anywhere else?"

"I've been here since. Is – how is – is Jasmine all right?"

"She'll live. Where's Daniel gone?"

"I don't know, I swear I don't know. But Jasmine, how's her –"

"We're not here to talk about Jasmine. We're here to talk about Daniel. We're here to work out where he's gone, and we're going to do that together. Do you think we can?"

"I don't know where he's gone – if he's not at home, I don't know."

"If you did, would you tell us?"

She hesitated. "Yes, I –"

"I don't believe you, love."

Her lips narrowed into a thin line. The blood drained from her face. "Have you, you could – have you asked his dad?"

"How long's it been now, Charlotte? It's been two weeks, hasn't it? More than. Now, you say you've been here since, so I'll assume you haven't heard much of what's been happening. But what do you think's been going on for the last fortnight? Do you think we've just been sitting on our hands?"

Charlotte sat wide-eyed like a rabbit in headlights.

Graeme drummed his fingers again. "Give us something to work with, pet."

"I don't have anything. I'm sorry."

"Try to think of something."

"There's nothing."

Graeme took a deep breath. He laced his fingers and popped his knuckles, let his eyes wander for a moment before settling them back on Charlotte. "How long have you been together, you and Dan?"

She frowned, the question unexpected. "Uh, um, about six, maybe seven months."

"How long have you known each other?"

"Years. Since school."

"Since school, eh? That's a lovely story. You leave school, a few years pass, and the two of you finally get together, decide to make a go of it. What'd you do for seven months? Alternate between his place and yours? You never took any trips? You never went to see friends outside of the group that were in the bar that night? Howay, pet, even Carl had been to his fucking uncle's house."

Charlotte swallowed.

"You're not trying hard enough, Charlotte. In fact, I don't think you're trying at all. You love him?"

"Uh, y-yes, yes. Yes, I do."

"That's lovely too. That's very nice. And it's sweet how you're trying to protect him, except you're not. You just think you are. If you know where he is, or if you've got any kind of idea where he could be, the best thing you can do is just tell us. The longer it takes, the worse it's gonna get. You understand that, don't you?"

"*Please*, I don't know where he is." Charlotte's eyes glistened.

Graeme leaned forward, pressed his thumbs into his face either side of his nose. He sighed. He sat back, let his head hang over the chair, his face turned to the ceiling. He made a big show of exasperation. He took deep breaths, then looked at her again.

"Where are your family, Charlotte?"

"What?"

"Your family. Mam, dad, little sister. I can see them there, in that picture." He pointed. "Your sister looks a fair bit younger than you. What is it, five, six years?"

Charlotte said nothing. She sat very still.

"She'll still be in school at that age, won't she? So you'll know where she is, day after day, between nine and three. She's at school. She walks there in the morning, she walks home in the afternoon. Mam and dad, what do they do? Come on pet, I'm asking – I'm genuinely curious over here."

"Uh – uh." She cleared her throat. "M-mam's a care worker – old people, at home. She goes to their homes. And dad's a mechanic."

"So mam does a lot of walking too, does she? Maybe a lot of driving. She'll have a schedule, won't she? Sees an old fella here, a dear wifey there. A route is as good as a workplace, isn't it? And dad's in the garage all day, so you know where he is, too. You always know where those closest to you are. Because you care about them, right? You wanna know where they are, because you want to know that they're safe."

Charlotte didn't blink.

"Except… You know what it is, love? I'm fifty-three now. I've known a lot of people, and I've seen a lot of things. And everyone loves someone. We've all got them people we care about, and we wanna keep them safe. Family, usually. When we're not with them, the only way we can rest easy is by knowing their whereabouts. You reckon that's so? We get this idea in our head that if we know where they are, they're all right. You see it on the news all the time, people lose their minds when someone they care about takes a wander, even if it's just for a day. They call the police, they call the news, they put out posters, they plead for them to come home.

"The thing is, no one's safe. At any time. Just because you know where they are doesn't mean you can do anything about it. Things are as out of your control when you know as when you don't. Your dad could be under a ramp one day, working on the underside of a car, and the hydraulics in the lift could go –" Graeme clapped his hands and Charlotte jumped. "He's crushed. Could you imagine that? Crushed under the weight of a car. Unless it snapped his neck first, when it went down. That would be for the best though, really. A quick death, rather than his breath being squeezed out of him, his crushed ribs tearing up his lungs and his guts. That would be an awful way to go.

"Cars are a hell of a thing. We take them for granted, but we forget just how dangerous they are. How prone they can be to fucking up on us, out of the blue, just like *that*." He clicked his fingers, Charlotte jumped again. She was trembling. Her watery eyes looked ready to spill over. "Your mam's driving along, she's in a rush because some old Mr has shit himself and she needs to get there to wipe his dry old arse for him, she's going a bit too fast and there's some traffic lights, so she hits the brakes. But then, the brakes don't work. The pipes have rusted, they've burst, brake fluid is pissing out all over the road and she's not getting any slower, she jams on the handbrake, swings the wheel, does everything she can to slow herself down, to avoid hitting the car stopped at the red, but all she does is lose control, flips the car, and I guess it all depends on how fast she was going but when does she stop rolling? And what state is she going to be in when she drags herself out – *if* she drags herself out. If she's lucky, just a couple of broken bones. But if she's *not*… Well, then she's the one gonna be needing a home visit, isn't she? She's the one gonna need someone to wipe her arse, to dry the spit on her chin. You could do it, eh? You could take that job.

Take good care of your dear old mam."

"Please…" Charlotte whimpered. Tears rolled down her face.

"Your sister. Baby sis. Bet she'll always be a baby to you, right?" Graeme smiled at her like they were remembering old times. "She's walking to school one morning, a Monday morning, let's say. Some careless prick is in his car and he really shouldn't be, because he stayed out late on Sunday night, took on a real skin-full, he's in no state to drive but he has to get to work, to the job he was drinking to forget the night before. He's not seeing straight. Keeps going over the white line. Then he's on the kerb. His eyes are closed, he's fallen asleep behind the wheel. His car goes up, it hits a bump, he gets that startled clarity that comes along every once in a while and he gets off the kerb, onto the road, he carries on his merry way and he never once looks back in the mirror to see what it was he hit. Doesn't look into the mirror to see the little girl lying dead on the pavement, her uniform all torn up, blood in her hair, her schoolbag dropped, exercise books blowing in the wind –"

"*Please –!*"

"Imagine, being all alone in the world. Your family just wiped out, and you're the only one left. But I bet you're the kind will visit their graves every week, leave fresh flowers. You'll never miss a visit. But you're gonna struggle, aren't you? Your whole world is going to fall apart. You'll have to learn how to cope, when you're visiting their graves and wondering if there's anything you could've done to prevent those accidents from happening. But there's not, love. You can't prevent accidents. They just happen. They happen every day."

Charlotte wept openly. Snot ran from her nose. She covered her face with her hands. Graeme let his words hang in the air, let them sink in.

"But the other thing, the thing that's not an accident, you can prevent that. You know you can. You just need to tell us what we want to know."

He gave her a moment.

"Tell us when you're ready, pet."

She tried to compose herself. Her sobs turned to hitching gasps, she wiped the tears from her eyes and sniffed hard. She cleared her throat. She calmed, but her breathing remained laboured, sounded like she was about to break down into tears again at any moment. "There's, there's a —" She closed her eyes, breathed deeply. "Up the coast. There's a small town, called Amble. There's a caravan site there. We went a couple of times. His uncle has one. We spent a few weekends."

"That's where he's gone?"

"I don't know."

"But you think it is?"

The tears came back. Charlotte closed her eyes. She nodded.

Graeme looked at Tony. Tony frowned back. He looked appalled. Graeme got to his feet, went to Charlotte. He patted her on the shoulder. She flinched beneath him. "Good lass," he said. "But if he's not there, we'll be back. Back to see what else you don't remember. All right? Don't plan any trips. Just think about your family, love."

9

They left the city. It was night time, dark. Tony drove. "You know where we're going?" he said.

"Aye," Graeme said. "I've been a couple of times."

"Much there?"

"Not really."

"Why you been?"

"Fishing."

"You fish?"

"Used to."

Graeme directed him onto the A1. They headed north. Tony had something to say, Graeme could tell. He was holding back.

"Just spit it out."

"Back there, with the young lass. That wasn't necessary."

"If you say so."

"Howay man, Graeme. That's not you."

Graeme snorted. "You don't know me like you think you do, Tony."

"That's not you."

"If you say so."

"For Christ's sake, man, Graeme!"

"Lookit, you wanna know what I am? Do you? I'm asking you here!"

"Yes! Yes I wanna know!"

"I'm the lesser of two evils, son. Anyone else went to see her, you know what they would have done? They wouldn't have talked. Aye, she's upset, and she's gonna be upset and scared for a while, but she can still walk. She can still write her own name, feed herself. And what's the downside? She's gonna hug her family a bit tighter for the next few months. It could have been worse."

Tony blew air through his nose. He didn't like it, but he wasn't going to argue about it, which to Graeme meant he had at least understood some of his explanation. When he did speak again, he said "How far away's it?"

"About half an hour, now."

"All right." Tony started thinking again. Graeme waited. "Here's a question then, about that lesser of two evils thing. We've got Paddy's phone. Why don't you just call Dan up, have a word with him?"

"Because that would spook him. He knows his uncle wouldn't give the phone up without a fight. We've got his uncle's phone, then he knows we've got his uncle. We've got his uncle, we've got his dad. He's got no one left. He'd shit himself and run, and we'd never fucking find him."

"Fair point. But here's another question. If Charlotte reckons this is where he's gone, if she misses him so much, why hasn't she just come up herself to meet him?"

"I don't know, Tony. Maybe she lied, maybe she has spoken to him, maybe this is exactly where he is or maybe it's the complete opposite."

"So another fuckin goose chase."

"Tony, like I said, I divvint fuckin kna, man. No one had been to see her yet, maybe she was just waiting for that, for it to finally come to her door so she could play dumb, send us off somewhere else, then head on up to be with him, happily ever after."

"Could be she has played dumb, and we're going the wrong way."

"Aye. Could be. I don't think so, though. You saw her. And the thing is, if he was swearing at her that night, trying to get rid of her, could be she's wary of coming up, of having the same thing happen again. Now, obviously I think he was doing that for her benefit, trying to keep her out of it, but when someone you love turns on you like that, it can mess with your head. You're not sure that they didn't mean it, and they don't wanna see you again."

Tony glanced over when Graeme went quiet. "You speaking from experience there?"

Graeme grunted. "You really wanna kna? It's about yer mother."

"Whey, probably I divvint mate, but so long as it's not rude, howay then."

"All right. I got back to your place pretty late one night, just kind of passed out on the bed next to your mam. In the morning, when there was a little more light, she saw something on me collar. She thought it was lipstick at first. She waited until you were off to school then she got ready to raise holy hell. Came and woke us up. Then she saw that them stains were round me cuffs, an'all. It was me own stupid fault, I was tired but I still should've taken the fucking shirt off. I'd done that, she wouldn't have noticed.

"The stains weren't lipstick. She realised that. They were blood. I'd tried to wash it off, probably that was why I didn't take the shirt off, thinking I'd done a better job than I actually had. But aye, it was blood on me collar and cuffs. She was still pretty fucking mad about it though. Thing is, she knew what I did. She'd always known. I never tried to hide it from her. I guess seeing the evidence of it, knowing it had slept next to her, that was too much. So, aye. That was when we mutually agreed to go our separate ways."

Tony was silent.

"It wasn't easy," Graeme said. "I loved your mam. Still do, I suppose. And I'd gotten pretty attached to you an'all, you little prick." Graeme grinned, but Tony just nodded. "But, well, you know we still get on. We got back in touch after a while. She told me about you. And when the time came you were looking for work, looking to move to the Toon, she gave me a call. Asked me to keep an eye out for you. Your mam loves you very much, Tony."

"Aye." Tony cleared his throat. "You, uh, did you…"

"What?"

"You missed her, aye?"

"Yeah. Course I did."

Through the dark, it looked as if Tony was gripping the steering wheel very tight. "So. Did you…"

"You know I did."

Tony drove. He stared straight ahead. He made no sign of acknowledgement.

It was after midnight when they reached Amble. They drove by the caravan site. It was gated. The caravans were mostly in darkness but a couple of them still had lights on. One hadn't bothered to close their curtains, and as they passed they could see the television playing in a corner of the small room. They had no idea which was Paddy's.

They drove to the town square, pulled into a car park, into deep darkness where there were no streetlights. Gravel crunched under their tyres. Tony killed the engine, and they settled back in their seats. Tony fell asleep almost instantly, but Graeme lay awake a while longer. He looked at Tony. Remembered him as a boy. Running, always out running, and when he wasn't running and his mother made him sit with them he was painfully shy. It had taken a long time for him to get comfortable around Graeme. A long time before he finally laughed at one of the bad jokes Graeme kept telling in an effort to win him over.

Time ticked by on the dashboard clock. Tony snored. Graeme closed his eyes, but for a long time it didn't make any difference. He kept them closed until finally sleep came, but by then it was almost dawn.

***

Graeme went to the site reception. Tony stayed in the car. The receptionist was a young lady with sleek black hair tied back into a bun. She was on the phone when he walked in. Graeme leaned on the counter, flashed his warmest smile. She returned it when she put the receiver down.

"Hello, pet," he said. "Now, this is pretty embarrassing, so promise us you won't laugh." He grinned sheepishly.

She grinned back. "All right then."

"I didn't hear you promise." He winked.

She laughed. "I promise."

"Okay. Well. Me mate's loaned us his caravan for a few days, but I've lost the directions for it. Now, I'd just give him a bell, y'kna, ask him meself, but I've lost me phone, too."

"That sounds careless," the receptionist said, but she was still smiling along. "What'll you lose next – the caravan?"

"Well, I bloody hope not! That's the kind of thing the fella isn't likely to forgive, I reckon."

"How'd you lose so much, anyway?"

"There may have been beer involved… Anyway, I was wondering if you could just point us in the right direction."

She pulled a face, like she wanted to but couldn't. Graeme had expected this. "I can't just give you the details. I'll have to call your friend first. What's his name?"

"It's Patrick. Patrick Moore."

She turned to her computer, typed the name in, checked files. "What's his home address?"

"His home address?" Graeme pulled a face, clicked his fingers. "Now you're askin, pet. It's a Byker address, unless he hasn't updated it."

"No, it's a Byker one."

"Grand. Is that enough?"

"It'll do." She winked. "I've just got to call him, to verify. What's your name?"

"It's Jeff Smith. Mind, I don't know what numbers you've got here, but I'd call his mobile. He'll be at work by now."

The receptionist nodded, then dialled the number. Graeme stepped away, left her to it, looked out the window to the wooden playground and climbing frame out front. There were no children playing on it. It was a school day. Beyond the playground he could see his car, and Tony on the phone. Tony took the phone from his ear and the receptionist called to Graeme.

"All right, Mr Smith." Graeme turned back to her. She was trying not to laugh.

"What'd he say?"

"Oh, I can't repeat it."

"Howay, tell us. Was it a bad word?"

"It certainly was."

"Howay, tell us what he said. I've heard them all before, pet. It'll stay between you and me."

"All right…he called you a 'dozy twat'."

Graeme laughed. "Aye, that sounds like Paddy."

"Okay then." She pulled out a site map. "This is

where we are." She circled them. "And this is where you need to be." She circled another area. "It's not far. Just follow the road."

Graeme took the map from her. "Grand. Cheers, pet!" He left, went back to the car, climbed in. He turned to Tony. "Dozy twat, eh?"

"She told you that, did she, Jeff?"

"Had to pry it out."

"Thought you'd like it."

"Made me day."

"Thought it'd sound like something Paddy might say."

"You're a real method actor. Anyway, this is where we're going." He held up the map. "Let's go. Left at the end there."

They turned left at the junction, past the showroom with a couple of bored-looking salespeople milling outside and sipping takeaway coffees, up the hill and along the road. Graeme looked out the window. "Take your time," he said. "Go slow. We're nearly there."

Tony slowed to a crawl, stopped when Graeme told him to. Graeme pointed through the caravans. Paddy's was next to the fence. Beyond it was a road, and beyond that were sand dunes that obstructed a view of the sea. A couple of windows were open, and a railing hung from one of them with drying clothes on it, swaying in the breeze.

"He's there," Tony said.

"It's not gonna be Paddy."

"What about them other caravans? Any signs of life?"

"Not much. I'd reckon it's a bit early in the season though, isn't it?"

"Haven't seen another moving car yet. What's our move?"

"We'll come back when it's dark. Just cos they look empty doesn't mean they are."

10

They killed time until midday, then went to the harbour, to a chip shop there. They sat on one of the benches down the side of the building and ate. There were clouds, but it wasn't raining and the air was warm. Seagulls circled at the sight of the food. Some of them landed, took cautious steps toward the bench. Graeme kicked a stone in their direction and they took flight, cawing. "Fuckin birds," he said.

"Horrible bastards," Tony said. He grimaced while he chewed, occasionally rubbed his jaw.

"Still hurts?"

"Everything hurts, mate. Y'kna, every time I see you lately I feel like I get me fucking face kicked in. Maybe once this is sorted, we leave it for a while, eh? Exchange Christmas cards and that'll have to do."

Graeme grunted, spiked a chip with his wooden fork. He had his fair share of aches and pains too, but compared to Tony he'd gotten off relatively lightly. When he was out the car, walking on the streets, he wasn't turning heads the way Tony was.

"I don't get hit this much when I'm on the doors."

"You must be on the wrong doors, then. Wasting your time."

"Aye, you say that, but you sorted it out."

"It's a cushy little number from what I heard."

"Aye. When I first got started, I thought I'd wanna

be where all the action was, y'kna? Thought I'd wanna be in the thick of it, getting stuck in. But I like it quiet. I don't mind a couple of drunks that just need steered in another direction, rather than having to give them an unnecessary clip round the lug."

Graeme looked into the distance while he chewed. There was a castle on a hill in the next town over. He looked at it for a long time, until Tony followed the line of his gaze.

"We're not here to sight-see, mate."

Graeme blinked, nodded. "Aye. I'm gonna have to ring Neil. Let him know."

"Set yourself away," Tony said. "I'm sure he'll be thrilled."

Graeme shovelled down a few more chips then pulled out his phone, found Neil's number. Neil answered promptly.

"We've got him."

"You've *got* him?"

"Not quite, but we know where he is."

"You've seen him?"

"No. But we're confident."

"You'd better be really fucking confident."

"We are."

"Divvint turn up empty-handed on me doorstep, mind. This needs to end."

"Aye."

"When're you gonna bring him in, then?"

"We'll get him tonight."

"Good. And lookit, I divvint care how late it is, bring him straight *here*. Bring him to me. I want him alive."

Graeme hesitated. "That necessary?"

Neil was silent for a moment. "*Necessary?*"

"Aye. Well, I mean, there's been a lot of bloodshed

already, Neil."

"You think I don't know that? This has gone on far too long now, *Graeme Taylor*."

Graeme realised what he'd said. "Sorry, but look, no one's listening in —"

"You know that for a fact, *Graeme Taylor*?"

"All right, all right, I get it, I'm sorry. I shouldn't have used your name, but howay man, after the last couple of weeks, I'm hardly gonna be grassing you up, am I?"

"Exactly. This bloodshed's on *your* hands, Graeme. Isn't that right? Paddy Moore, bludgeoned with the hammer?"

Graeme put his head in his hands. "Christ's sake, man, I said I get it, I get it. But listen, the point I was trying to make was, it was an accident. Originally, I mean. Daniel with your young'un. The dart. And there's been a shitload of mess for an *accident*."

Neil was quiet. When he spoke finally, his voice was restrained, like he was spitting the words through gritted teeth, trying not to shout. "He needs to be punished. He needs to *suffer*. I don't care if it was a fucking *accident*. My kids...it's all down to that cocksucker."

"I know it's only been a day, but any news on Michael?"

Neil's tone softened, but just barely. "No change. Nothing yet." He inhaled sharply. "Right, I want that lad gift-wrapped by tomorrow morning at the latest. You got that?"

"Aye."

Neil hung up. Graeme bit his lip.

Tony saw the look on his face. "What?"

Graeme shook his head. "Nowt."

"Don't give us that, man. What'd he say?"

"Just the usual. He's dying to get his hands on this

kid."

"And you're finally bothered about what he's going to do once he has him."

"I've always been bothered."

"You've done a bloody good job of hiding it."

"I hide a lot of things very well."

Tony looked like he wanted to say more, but he decided against it.

"What?"

"Nothing."

"*What*, man?"

"*Nowt*, man."

They ate in silence.

11

They waited until after midnight, when it was dark and there were few cars on the roads and even fewer people. With luck, Daniel would be sleeping.

Neither man spoke as Tony drove to the site, let the wheels roll slowly, carrying them up the hill and to Paddy's caravan. The night was clear. There was a full moon. Graeme watched it, watched the way it lit buildings and ground, yet made the shadows between appear all the darker.

"He's there," Tony said.

The caravan door was open. A kid sat on the steps, smoking. It was Daniel. It had to be. Graeme conjured up the image of the photograph in Charlotte's flat, tried to compare the two, but it was dark and hard to tell.

But Daniel saw the car, saw it stop. The cigarette had been halfway to his mouth. It dangled midair.

"He's seen us," Tony said.

"Has to be him, then," Graeme said. "Fuckin has to be."

Daniel stood.

"*Shit*," Graeme said.

Daniel jumped off the steps. He ran.

"Cut across the grass," Graeme said.

Tony mounted the kerb, put his foot down and sped across the grass between the caravans. Daniel scaled the fence. Tony skidded to a halt and jumped out, gave chase. Graeme followed.

Daniel dropped down the other side as Tony started climbing. Daniel sprinted over the road, toward the beach. Tony cleared the fence, followed. Graeme got to the fence, put his fingers tentatively to the mesh. "Shite," he said. He looked left and right, checked for a gate, but if there was one it was too far away. He braced himself and started to climb. It had been a long time since he'd last climbed anything, and whenever that might have been he was surely a lot younger and a lot lighter. He watched Tony run Daniel down atop the dunes, watched him tackle him into the sand, struggle with him in the long, sharp grass, put his hand over his mouth to muffle his screams and shouts. Graeme reached the top, sucking air. He put a leg down, tried to get his footing, slipped and fell.

He landed hard on the grass. The air was knocked out of him. He gasped and groaned, then rolled onto his front and pushed himself up. He stumbled over the road, onto the dunes. Tony had Daniel pinned to the ground, a knee in his back. The kid was crying.

"Get him up," Graeme said. "Give him here."

Tony hoisted Daniel up, kept tight hold of him as he handed him over. Graeme put an arm around Daniel's shoulders, held him close.

"Let's have a seat, eh?"

They sat down together. Daniel whimpered. "*Please*," he said. "I'm sorry, I'm so sorry – I didn't mean it –"

"I know you didn't, son, I know you didn't." He patted his arm. "But right now I just need a seat. That climb didn't half take it out of us. I'm not a young man like you two, y'kna."

Behind them, Tony remained standing, watchful

should Daniel tried to make a break for it. Graeme held him tightly, squeezed him to his body.

"Look out at the sea there," Graeme said. "Breathe it all in. Isn't that beautiful?"

The moon reflected on the black water. Its illumination made the sand below them look brilliantly clean, almost white, like something in a tropical country. In the distance there was a small rock island, a lighthouse upon it.

"That really is something, isn't it? The kind of thing they've probably got printed on a thousand fucking postcards in every gift shop throughout this tiny town. You reckon so? Maybe you know so. You've been here longer than we have. We just came up for the day." Graeme looked out, took in the sight. He took a deep breath through his nose, felt himself smile. He couldn't remember the last time he'd been to the beach, whether at night or day.

"Now listen to us, son. I know what you did was an accident. Tony here knows it. Jasmine knows it, and even her dad knows it, really. But he wants blood. He wants your blood. That's just the kind of man he is. He's cut from the same cloth as your dad and uncle, so I know you understand. And listen, speaking of them two, they're dead. All right? I'm sorry to break it to you like this, but when it comes to death there's never really an easy way to tell someone."

Graeme could feel Daniel's hot tears soaking through his shirt. He pulled him closer. Daniel cried harder.

"But your lass, Charlotte, aye? She's all right. Take solace in that. She misses you, she's worried about you, but she's all right."

Daniel whimpered.

"Now listen, I'm gonna tell you a little story before

we get going. I remember, way back when, long before Doyle had reinvented himself as the businessman he is today, he was just known around town as a rowdy little bastard always looking for a fight. Me and him had it out on the cobbles a few times, but he was such a mousy little cunt I don't think there were many round Tyneside at that time that didn't go at least one round with him. Back then, I was pretty mousy meself. Gave as good as I got. I think he respected that, and he still does. He hasn't forgotten I put him down a couple of times.

"See, Doyle's a nasty bastard. Like all nasty bastards, he's a bit of a bully, too. Shite man, you don't need me telling you all this, you could probably guess for yourself. You've just gotta spend five minutes in a room with the bloke to work out what kind of man he is. Anyway, if you went toe-to-toe with him and you couldn't handle yourself, he'd pick you apart. He'd take his time. He'd really get into it, really enjoy himself. The fellas he fought, he wouldn't knock them down. He'd bloody them. Break their noses. Blacken their eyes. Knock out their teeth and burst their eardrums. He'd get off on it."

Daniel squirmed still. He shook. Any words he might have tried to speak were muffled against Graeme's chest.

"You might think he'd mellow with age, but he hasn't. He's as bad now as he ever was. Sometimes I think he's worse. And when it comes to the well-being of his kids, I know he is. He's a hard man, and he's not given much to sentiment, but when it's his kids, or his wife, well – perhaps it's love for them that drives him to protect them, or avenge them. But I'm not sure. He's always been proprietal. If it's his, you'd better not want it, and you'd better not harm it.

"So anyway, here's a for instance. Back in the day,

when he was still fighting and before Michael was born, before Michael's mother was on the scene, there was another woman. Rebecca Armstrong. You'll not know the name, I don't expect you to, I couldn't even tell you where she is these days. I remember her, though. She had this long black hair, dyed obviously, and this horrible fucking orange colour to her skin. I didn't think she was anything special, but she was the kind of lass that did herself up to get paraded round town on the arm of the local hard man, and some people go in for that kind of thing. Doyle did. Went in for her big time. Everywhere he went, there she was. And he was showing her off, putting her in all these tight dresses he'd buy for her, designer tags and the like, and she'd be dripping with all this garish fucking jewellery. And Rebecca loved it, she loved the life he gave her, but you know what else she loved? All the attention she got from the boys eyeing her up when Doyle was showing her off. Wanted to have her cake and eat it. And for a while she did, until Doyle found out she was fucking another lad — don't ask us how he found out, I don't know. He was so mad it didn't seem like the best thing to question at the time. Anyway, he wanted me to go find this lad, I can't remember his name, it was something like Booth — we'll say it was Booth. So I asked round and I tracked Booth down at his flat in Gateshead, gave him a clip and brought him in. I've been doing Doyle's dirty work for a very long time now. That was the start of it.

"Now, it'd be naïve of me to say I didn't think Doyle wasn't gonna hurt the lad. I knew he was. I knew he was gonna do bad things to him. But I didn't know how bad. Doyle was embarrassed by the whole incident, and that spurred him on as much as anything else. So I took Booth to Doyle, and Doyle strapped the lad to a chair, and I stayed there with some other blokes and we watched, and for two fucking days Doyle took Booth apart – and I do mean that fucking *literally* – for two days he destroyed this lad's body. Kept him alive, too. Every time it looked like he was about to bleed out, he'd tie him off, clean him up, get him a glass of water.

"Booth begged, he pleaded, he apologised – and in the end he just prayed for it to end. And it did end, eventually. Everything ends. It's just the getting there that's the hard part. Doyle slit his throat. Bright fucking red with this kid's blood, he took a knife and opened his neck and got covered in some more of it. That's the only kind of mercy you get from a man like Neil Doyle, the kind you have to suffer for first."

Graeme took a deep breath. He watched the lighthouse. Daniel was still.

"And that was over some woman he'd already kicked to the kerb. It was his pride, y'see. He'd been mugged off, and he couldn't allow that, so he made a big show in front of me and a few others, and made it very clear not to fuck with him in any way, shape, or form. That was a long time ago. People forget these things. A lot of the other men in that room with us, they're either dead, in prison, or abroad. The dead don't care, and the ones that have moved on or gotten themselves locked up, they can afford to forget what Doyle did to Booth, either because they've got some new problems, or they've done their best to run away from it all. Every generation needs a reminder of who's in charge, and that's what this is. He's letting everyone know, if you harm his property, he's coming after you, and you'd better have the fuckin dogs of Hell at your back, because nowt's gonna stop him. Jasmine doesn't want this, son. Nobody wants this but Doyle. And he's gonna take you in a room, strap you to a chair, and he's gonna take you apart an inch at a time, and he's gonna make sure there's plenty folk around to see it."

Graeme stopped talking. He stayed silent for a long time, until finally Tony said, "Come on, Graeme. Let's just get him back."

Graeme let his arm fall from Daniel's shoulders. Daniel stayed slumped against him like he'd fallen asleep. Tony reached for him, then flinched and snatched his hand back as if he'd been burnt.

"He's dead," he said.

"Aye," Graeme said.

He looked out across the water, at the moon above, the innumerable stars around it. He sat for a long time, the dead body pressed to his side.

12

Neil sat behind his desk, his chin in his hand and a finger curled around his mouth. "Killed himself," he said.

"Aye." Graeme sat on the sofa. He was alone. He'd sent Tony home. "We went into the caravan, he'd hanged himself from a light fixture."

"Did he see you coming?"

"No. Judging by the smell, the state of the place, he'd been there a while."

Neil's jaw worked. "All right. Well." He took a deep breath through his nose, sat up straight. "Lad seemed like a pussy anyway. Can't say I'm massively surprised he'd take the easy way out."

"No."

"The body?"

"Left it."

"Cover your tracks?"

"Of course."

"Good. These things should go without saying, but a lot of these lads these days, y'kna what they're like."

"You can count on me."

Neil nodded once. "Aye."

Jasmine was in the hallway as Graeme left. She'd been to the kitchen, carried a bottle of water and a packet of crisps. She wore the same dressing gown as the last time he'd seen her, but it looked like she'd changed the pyjamas.

Her eye locked on Graeme for just a moment, then she looked away and went up the stairs. As she reached for the banister the first time she missed, brushed it with her fingertips, had to grab for it again, gripped it angrily. She blew air through her nose, grit her teeth, kept a tight hold on the railing as she made her way up.

***

Graeme went home. He parked his car and sat in it for a while. The grey clouds hung so low they almost touched the top of his building. His stomach grumbled and he thought about going along to the café, to see Shannon, but he didn't do it. He went inside instead, trudged up the stairs to his flat, stepped inside and stood in the silence. He probed his face where it still held the lingering pains of Paddy's punches.

His hands began to shake. He stopped them. He went to his room and sat on the edge of the bed. Everything was quiet. Everything was still. Everything was just as he'd left it. He took a deep breath through his nose, and when he exhaled it almost sounded like a sigh. All of a sudden he was acutely aware of the loneliness of his living situation. Painfully aware.

There was a knock at his door. He didn't get off the bed, just turned his head toward the sound. There was another knock, harder this time, and he heard a voice call through. "Howay, Graeme mate. You home?" It was Tony.

Graeme answered. "Wasn't expecting to see you."

Tony carried a six-pack of beers in one hand and a bag of takeaway in the other. It smelled like Chinese. "I took the night off," he said. "I figured I've been missing so many shifts lately, fuck it. I'll miss one more. And they got that two week stretch in the middle there. That was completely unmarred by outside illness. So really, they can't complain."

"Nah, they can't complain."

"You gonna invite us in, then, or what?"

Graeme led him through to the kitchen. Tony dumped the bag in the middle of the small round table there while Graeme grabbed a couple of plates and cutlery. He took a seat and opened a beer.

"Bit early in the day, isn't it?"

"Probably a bit early for Chinese food an'all," Tony said. "I'm throwing all caution to the wind."

Graeme took a seat. "There not somewhere you'd rather be?"

Tony shrugged. "Like where?"

"I dunno. You seem pretty attached to the gym, like."

"Gotta take a break from that place every once in a while."

"So I hear."

Tony forked rice onto his plate, poured curry over the top of it, then slid the carton towards Graeme. He was about to start eating but then he stopped, hesitated. "You heard anything about Michael?"

"You concerned about him, like?"

"I'm curious."

"Just what I was told yesterday. Safe to assume there's no change."

"How's Neil feel about that?"

"I didn't ask."

"Because you don't wanna know?"

"Something like that."

Tony put his fork down. "Lookit. I got to thinking. Neil, y'kna, he *might've* gone and seen his son in the hospital, I don't know that he didn't, but it was like…like…I dunno, man. It was like that wasn't the first thing on his mind, y'kna? Or Jasmine, either. It was more that he felt insulted there'd been a slight made against *him*. Y'kna?"

"Yeah."

"It just doesn't…that doesn't sit right. Not with me. I feel kind of…I feel kind of shit for them, for the kids. Both of them. I mean, Jasmine's got this reputation as a spoilt brat, and it's probably warranted, but I reckon buying her all that shit, intimidating people that piss her off, that's more for him, you reckon? I'm just thinking out loud here. You reckon that's just him showing off?"

"Could be."

"Anyway. Anyway. Forget it. That's not what I was thinking about. I was remembering after me and Michael had the straightener, and I had me fucking nose spread all over me face and I was laid up in bed feeling like I had a fractured fucking skull. You remember that?"

"Aye. You didn't half milk it." Graeme grinned.

"Fuck off, man. I'd like to see you bounce back any quicker."

"I'm an old man. Not young and sprightly like yourself."

"Aye, whey. You came to see us, didn't you? That helped. Getting the shopping in and that. Heating up them soups. You didn't have to do any of that."

"I didn't mind."

"It doesn't matter if you didn't mind, you didn't have to do it, y'kna? And I was still pissed off at you, because I thought you were balls-deep with Doyle, and cos I'm always made to feel like I owe you something. And I don't just mean by you, me mam does me fucking head in with it, always banging on about you. But, because I was pissed off and all the rest of it, I never told you I appreciated it. When you came round. I appreciated it."

"It's all right," Graeme said.

Tony nodded. "Aye."

Graeme opened a beer and they tapped cans. Tony started eating. Graeme watched him until Tony noticed and looked up, then he turned away. He still needed to plate his food. He looked through the kitchen window at the grey and dirty day outside, looked to the city until, finally, he felt he could close his hot eyes.

"You gonna cry?" Tony said.

Graeme grinned. "No."

"You look like you're gonna cry."

"I'm not."

"Good. Divvint gan getting soft on us, you big tart."

Printed in Great Britain
by Amazon

86642705R00071